THE LAST SIREN

T.G. Sparks

BLUE FORGE PRESS
Port Orchard, Washington

*For the kid who needed to know they weren't broken.
It took a little while but hey, we figured it out.*

Acknowledgments

Wow! There are so many people to thank! First off, thank you to my parents. Without you, I would have never had the energy to write this. Thank you for everything you do for me and thank you for supporting me in this journey. Thank you for letting me make this leap.

To my sibling, thank you for not bugging me while I was working!

To my grandmother, thank you so much for supporting me.

A big thank you to my teachers. I'm sorry for writing this while I was supposed to be paying attention in your class. Especially, thank you to my ELA teacher for reading the first mess of a draft.

Thank you to Blue Forge Press. This has been a wonderful journey and you have been lovely to work with. It has been an honor to publish with you.

Thank you to everyone who has given me feedback on this as it has existed in all of its various forms: my mom, my teachers, and especially my friends from camp. I take all of your feedback into consideration and the things you have told me have shaped this story into what it is today.

Lastly, a massive thank you to all of my beta readers: Mary, Shannon, Kim, and Ivy. You caught so many things I would have missed. Your help has been priceless. Thank you so, so much.

Writing this novel has been a really transformative experience, and I am very excited to see where it goes in the world.

And to you, the reader. I hope you enjoy *The Last Siren*.

THE LAST SIREN

T.G. Sparks

CHAPTER 1

H ali hissed in annoyance, struggling to stay standing as her legs almost gave out. *Why the gods is walking so hard?* she thought. *Couldn't I have gotten, I don't know, a seagull to help me out?*

She tried to keep her balance, hoping to ignore the concerned glances she received. If anyone acted on their concern, it would cause a lot of problems she didn't have the time to handle. Having legs wasn't usual for her, so naturally, she was bad at using them. She wanted her tail back. It was so much more useful.

If it were for any other reason, she wouldn't have come up here. The land was a danger zone for someone like her. But while she had been wallowing in her own pity, she had been trapped by the giant gate-wall thing the king had built around the island. She had tried living on her own underwater for a few months, but it just wasn't working. She was lonely. So, so lonely. Abandoned cities are only fun to explore once. She needed out. And to get out she needed someone to take her. Luckily, she had found someone willing to smuggle her over the wall. Unluckily, he had only agreed to meet in a pub in the main port.

That was how Hali found herself walking through the harbor of a kingdom that would have her executed if the dark blue hood she had pulled over her head flew off. Or if someone looked a little too close at her uncovered feet.

Transforming into a human didn't hide all of her siren features. Patches of blue and green scales remained on her legs and arms, and her eyes were a dead giveaway. The hood hid her ears well, which was good; if they were seen she would never be able to lie her way out.

She took in the wood buildings, feeling a sense of familiarity in the town. The thatched roofs with the stone castle looming over it was a sight she had fond memories of from the rare occasions her mother had brought her up here, or when she snuck up with a friend. It was the beginning of summer, but the kingdom remained cold. It never got that warm in Carnelian, both underwater and above. The women were all wearing shawls and thick petticoats. The men were all bundled in thick cloaks and trousers. Hali didn't have any of those things, leaving her at the mercy of the cold. She was wearing thin brown trousers, a thin white tunic, and a dark blue cape with a hood. She hadn't been able to find the pair of shoes she had stashed so the cold stone streets froze her toes.

Hali stumbled down the street, opting to lean against the walls and pretend she was drunk. It didn't look too far off. She rolled her eyes at all the disgusted looks people gave her, but was glad no one assumed anything else. That seemed to work, but she still couldn't shake the feeling of a million eyes on her. People were watching, and she knew people were perceptive. Part of it was paranoia, yes, but she was paranoid for good reason. No one would figure the truth out. She was a good actor, and the whole kingdom thought all the sirens were gone. Yet another part felt real. There were many people on the street, someone had to notice her. Someone had to see, and they still hadn't said anything.

It took her a little while to reach her destination, but eventually, Hali found herself standing in front of the Swan and Dolphin pub. It was a small building, made of wattle and daub with a straw roof. The sign was ornate and made of colored metal, depicting a swan with its neck wrapped around a dolphin surrounded by thorns. She could hear music and yelling coming from inside.

Opening the door, she was assaulted by the smell of alcohol. She scrunched up her nose and entered the small pub. The back wall was the main bar, an ornate counter with a large mirror and racks of booze. There were tables in the center, occupied by groups of very drunk sailors. Circular booths were built into the walls where illegal activity was obviously happening but no one cared.

She made her way through the crowd, ducking around the sailors and bar patrons who were too drunk to watch out for her, and took a seat at one of the booths towards the back. Across from her was a greasy man with blonde hair and stubble. He was wearing a black cape that completely concealed his physique. Hali found that made her a bit nervous. He could have concealed weapons, and she would be totally unprepared when he attacked her. Not that he was going to attack her, but she didn't have a lot of confidence in him. He was a shady individual after all.

As she sat down she adjusted her stature to make herself appear older, sitting straighter than she normally would and tilting her chin up. If she was going to get what she needed, she had to appear intimidating. Her old friend, Marni, had taught her that early on when they were teaching her how to get illegal goods and services. *Wow,* she thought. *Marni was a terrible influence, weren't they?*

"You said you could take me. Tell me the plan," Hali demanded, not making eye contact with her informant. She cursed how she sounded. She was trying to be intimidating but it wasn't working with her dolphin voice.

The man grunted. "I've got tickets on The Burnet, one of the passenger ships leaving port in five days. I'll do the talking, you stand behind me and keep your head down. After the ship passes the gates, you jump off and be on your merry way. Go wherever you are planning on going and all that. Not my problem. So, we got a deal?"

Hali nodded. "I'll pay you when we get on the ship."

"No. Half now," he grunted.

Hali glared. "No. I pay when we get on the ship. I'm not letting you just run away as soon as I give you the money."

The man smirked. "Y'know, I could just turn you in to the knights right now. The bounty for sirens is still in effect, and It's quite a lot more than you're willing to give me. So I'd play your cards carefully."

Hali winced. He was right. Sighing, she opened her satchel of coins and pulled out a handful of gold medallions with the kingdom's crest, a crown with a mountain behind it, imprinted on them, and slid the pile to the man in the cloak. He inspected them, counting them slowly. Hali watched with impatience.

"Alright," the man said, standing up briskly. "Meet me here in seven days at dusk. We'll leave then." And with that, he turned around and stalked out of the pub.

Well. That was quick. Hali looked around, eyeing the food on the other tables hungrily. She once again opened her coin satchel to count what was left. She hadn't brought all of her money with her, that would have been a stupid thing to do. She had a stash in the place she was staying. Unfortunately, she was very much out of money, with one measly coin left. Definitely not enough for food from the pub.

Sighing, she stood up and made her way out of the pub, the loud noise of drunk patrons faded away as she closed the door behind her. But the noise didn't exactly fade away, only became replaced by the hustle and bustle of a port town. It wasn't an uncommon noise, ports of trade were always busy. But for Hali, the noise was a stark contrast to the quiet of the ocean cities. It was comforting. Months of suffocating silence make any kind of chatter feel like a godsend. She relished in it. The comforting marketplace noise made her feel at home, even as she walked through a kingdom that would never welcome her.

The marketplace sold a variety of things, mainly fruits and vegetables. There was a small stand that sold hand-carved figures. Hali stopped to look at them but kept walking when she saw a figure of a siren poised to attack.

The crowd consisted of peasants who were just here for the necessities. There were nobles here, though, easily noticeable by their fine clothes, as well as sailors, with their rugged appearance and the red sash they wore around their arms, signaling they were citizens of Carnelian. Both groups had gathered around a specific stall, the one where the vendor called out "Charms to ward off sirens! Get them here!"

She sped past that one and made sure her hood was securely up.

Hali looked up, hearing something she wasn't at all expecting. "Look! It's the princess!" someone said.

Hali stiffened. She looked around and found herself staring at the princess of Carnelian, who was walking down the street, taking in the sights as if she was just a normal passerby. A million thoughts ran through her head but one stuck out in particular. *Oh, gods, she's hot.* That was not at all what she was expecting to think, but Hali had to admit it was true. She couldn't deny the facts. She did look very confident and strong in her white tunic with a blue unbuttoned vest and brown leather pants with boots. She shook her head, shaking that thought away. *We'll deal with this later. On another note, what on earth is she doing here? I could maybe live if some townsperson gave me pity if they caught me but the princess? If she sees me, I'm dead.*

There wasn't a way to avoid passing her. Hali was trapped in between buildings with the princess blocking the way back to the small beach alcove she had used to get here in the first place. And the crowd was steadily growing and crowding behind her. So, Hali started walking forward. She stayed at the edge of the street, watching as the princess with the cute freckles got closer and closer. Then, of all the things that could go wrong, the princess started walking in her direction.

Hastily, Hali started trying to get closer to the buildings. So hastily in fact, that she bumped into someone. She bounced back, and the person scowled at her, luckily not paying much attention. "Watch it," they grumbled before turning back to the vendor they were chatting with.

"Sorry!" Hali stammered, turning quickly to try and walk away, only to run directly into the one person she was trying desperately to avoid.

The princess.

The princess tumbled backward, Hali following suit. They landed in a very compromising position, with Hali sprawled on top of the royal. Hali was able to slightly catch herself, still leaving their faces almost touching. The other girl's eyes widened. "Y-you..." she stammered.

Hali quickly rolled off her, feeling complete and utter terror but knowing better than to remain *on top* of the princess. Who, by the way, had a sword. After that, she was frozen. Sitting on the frosty ground. Luckily, her hood was still up. The princess stood. Her long, light brown hair fell in her face as her pale blue eyes widened in confusion. Anger started to take over her features, and Hali winced back and waited for the inevitable call that would seal her fate. And then, the craziest thing happened. She smiled. A soft, amused smile that made Hali's insides feel fuzzy. The princess offered her a hand. "Here, let me help."

Now it was Hali's turn to be confused. She cocked her head to the side. "What?" she managed to stutter out.

The princess looked around, and when she noticed people were starting to stare she shooed them off roughly. Hesitantly, Hali grabbed her hand and the princess pulled her up. She grabbed her elbow roughly, making Hali freeze in fear. The princess saw this and sighed in frustration. "Look. I'm not going to hurt you. I'm just surprised you're up here."

Hali glared back, feeling her courage return. "Well there's a wall around my home, no thanks to you, so of course, I'm trying to get out. I need to be up here to do that."

The brown-haired girl looked down. Her expression was frustrated and guilty. "I'm sorry," she mumbled.

Then, as if that moment hadn't happened at all, she was back to glaring. Though, now Hali could see the layers of something else buried under it. Concern.

"Just, be careful, okay? You're being incredibly risky just being here and while I'm going to let you go if it had been anyone else that you bumped into you wouldn't have been so lucky."

Hali shook her arm off. "You actually think I don't know that?" she whispered, still glaring. "I'm fine. I know what I'm doing. You don't need to worry about me." And with that, she walked off, leaving the stunned princess behind her. The bit about her knowing what she was doing was a lie, but the princess didn't need to know that.

She kept walking, trying to shake away the memory of her weird interaction with the beautiful princess. *Well, now I'm not as crazy for thinking she's pretty. At least she's not trying to kill me.* Hali stumbled towards the docks, weaving her way through the people as best she could.

She was just minding her own business when all of a sudden a small child ran straight into her legs with a crash. She didn't fall all the way, but unfortunately, her hood flew off. Everything stopped. People all turned to stare. The little kid backed away slowly. Hali froze. *Welp,* she thought. *There goes my cover.*

Finally, someone broke the silence. "Siren!" they yelled. That was enough to spur Hali into movement, and she took off at a full sprint to the edge of the dock. She wasn't gracefully sprinting—she looked more like a drunk horse than a person—but it was at least working. Behind her, more people shouted, some of them calling for the knights. That only made her go faster.

She dodged and weaved through the dock hands who were unloading a shipment of something in boxes from one of the sailing ships.

The water came quickly, its dark blue depths drawing her in. She was a child of the ocean after all, and it would always be welcoming for them. Hali felt its call, and in one motion jumped off the edge of the dock and plunged into its freezing depths.

CHAPTER 2

Princess Audra of Carnelian definitely had a temper. She got frustrated easily, especially when people were stubborn. Currently, she was extremely frustrated at the incredibly stupid, stubborn, admittedly cute siren she had seen in the market.

She had left the market soon after the encounter, the entire conversation had ruined the point of being down there in the first place. Seeing the people—her people—so happy was enough to ease her guilt, if only for a little while. When her father started killing the sirens, she tried to fight him. But her father didn't like that. After a while, he issued a proclamation that said that any order she gave was completely invalid. Privately, he had threatened to remove her from the line of succession. She couldn't have that. If that happened, the next in line was her greedy uncle who would drive the kingdom into the ground. So, she kept quiet.

She tried to tell herself she was doing the right thing, but that guilt of seeing an entire pod slaughtered was still eating at her. The Evergreen Sea Pod had its own government system but still considered itself part of Carnelian. They were still her people. She had failed them. But she pushed that guilt down and kept quiet, silently waiting for her father's reign to end and for her time to take up the throne. *At least,* she thought, *there are no sirens left for him to hurt.*

But then she had quite literally run into that siren in the market, and now her mind was a mess. She hadn't even thought of the possibility that there could be more sirens still out there. And then out of the blue, she met one. Now, she didn't know what to do or what to feel.

She sighed and kept walking through the stone hallways of the castle. The curved windows on one side let light in, so torches weren't needed. They would be lit when the sun started to set. No one was in this part of the hallway, as none of the rooms were in use. Well, they were rarely used. Audra actually spent quite a lot of time in the room behind the wooden double doors at the end of the hallway.

Speaking of which, Audra had finally reached the doors. She pushed the left one open, revealing the massive library of a bedroom within. Her mother's bedroom. The inside was round, and all of the walls were completely covered in bookshelves except for a fireplace opposite the main entrance. A large bed with light pink drapes and blankets sat in the middle of the room. Audra knew somewhere in the room was a secret door that opened up to a walk-in closet. The only other furniture in the room was two worn-looking leather armchairs.

Audra smiled, closing the door behind her. This had been her safe place within the palace ever since she could remember. There was an edge of bitterness about it now, but also a comforting presence.

Audra had been seven when her mother died. Queen Calia had been a kind and gentle leader. She was wise and strong. But to Audra, she had always just been Mother, the nice parent who would sit in one of the armchairs and stroke her hair while reading a story. She was also the only parent ever around. Her father was always too busy with the king's work. He still was. Audra always thought it was a shame that her mother had married him. It had been a political match, a marriage to secure an alliance between the kingdom of Carnelian and the cold lands which had recently been conquered. Her mother didn't deserve her father. She deserved someone better. Someone who truly loved her as a person, and not as a prop.

She shook her head, dispelling those thoughts as she sank into one of the armchairs. As she daydreamed, she remembered a conversation she had had in this very chair many years ago. She was probably only about five at the time, still too young to really understand the meaning of her mother's words.

"Mommy?" she had asked. Her mother hummed, not looking up from her book. There were no windows in the room, so the only light came from the fireplace. The flames made her mother's blonde hair seem like it was glowing, and her chestnut eyes reflected their intricate dance. She was a slim woman, with delicate features and a pale complexion, compliments of being a noble from the now-fallen cold lands to the north. She wore a long silk nightgown, as it was late in the evening.

"Yes?" she said.

"Why does Daddy not like the sirens? Milos is a siren and he's nice," Audra asked. Milos had been a 'friend' of the queen's. At least, that's what Audra and the rest of the kingdom were told. Looking back on it, Audra could very clearly see that her mother was having an affair with him. And to be completely honest, Audra didn't blame her. Her father never showed any kind of affection while Milos showered her with it.

The queen smiled. "Your father just doesn't like things he doesn't understand. He's afraid of them."

Audra's face scrunched up in confusion. "That's stupid. If he doesn't understand he should learn."

Her mother laughed lightly, a kind sound that made Audra's heart clench at the memory of it. "I'm glad you've found a solution. But, unfortunately, it's not that simple. Your father is stuck in his ways and won't admit to being wrong." She paused, and for the first time in their conversation took her eyes off her book. "Audra," she said very seriously. "I need you to promise me something."

Audra felt confused but nodded anyway. "What is it?"

"I need you to promise me that you'll always do what you think is right. You're a strong girl, stronger than you know, and you should never let anyone take away your voice." The queen extended her pinky finger, leaning closer to Audra's younger self. A pinky promise. Childish, yes, but she was making a promise with a child.

Audra smiled and wrapped her finger around her mothers, sealing the promise. "I promise," she said with as much certainty as her tiny five-year-old self could muster. Her *mother giggled and then went back to her book.*

Audra blinked. She hadn't thought about that promise in a long time. She hadn't even remembered it before coming here today. *Well,* she thought, *I've broken that promise. I hope Mother will understand, though. I hope they all will.*

There was a knock at the door, startling Audra out of her thoughts. That was surprising, as people rarely came down this hallway. "Come in!" Audra called.

The door opened slowly, and Audra released a breath she didn't even know she was holding at the sight of her personal servant, Lila. She was on the smaller side, with blonde hair and green eyes. Her cheeks were dusted with freckles, more than Audra had. Her hair was always kept in a tight bun. She wore a long green dress that had a few patches here and there and an apron. "Milady," she greeted in her thick accent. Audra had never actually asked where Lila was from, but she definitely had a dialect from wherever it was. She spoke with a definite drawl, one Audra had only ever heard in sailors from the south. Lila continued. "It's your father. He's wantin' to speak with you. He doesn't look very happy."

Audra stood up at that. It was extremely rare for her father to ask for her. And if he was mad it usually was going to end in a fight. Seeing as it was best not to keep him waiting, Audra muttered a quick "thank you" to Lila before making her way to her father's office.

Lila hated her king. Actually, no. She refused to call him *her* king. *The* king. Lila hated the king. There were so many reasons she could list. The fact that despite Carnelian being a fairly wealthy company she was paid almost nothing by him. Audra paid her and many other workers more in secret. There was his blatant disregard for anyone working. He would storm through the palace and push anyone out of his way. And none of this was even touching on the whole siren debacle. That was a whole pile of dung she didn't even want to get into right now.

Lila wasn't someone who was quick to anger. She had been raised right and proper, well mostly. She was a good girl. Sweet and kind to a T. But the king made all the rage she kept close to her chest fill her mind. She might be a good girl, but she had rage and righteousness in her blood.

And now, watching Audra walk through the halls of the palace, she was reminded of every grievance she had with that rotten man. Audra was like the younger sister she never had. The gods had led Lila to her and she couldn't be more thankful. Audra had such a bright soul, and it hurt Lila's heart to see her turn off that light—because if she didn't, Audra's father would try to squash it.

So yes, Lila hated the king. But more than that, she hated how he treated Audra.

There wasn't much she could do for now, honest. As much as it pained her, she couldn't stop Audra from making her way to that cold office of his. It was a scary room, Lila would admit. Though she didn't know how much of that was the office itself or just that the king was there. She certainly didn't like to go there. She could imagine Audra didn't either.

She all but ran back to Audra's chambers, a smile sweet with poison plastered on her face. There was a time for anger, and that time was outside of work hours. While she couldn't stop Audra from being hurt, she could make the aftermath the best it could be. Audra would come back to her room to find it perfectly clean, with the pillows fluffed and an extra blanket on her bed. She would come back to a spotless room, she would. Lila would make sure of it.

It didn't take Audra long to get where she was going. Most of the rooms used by the royal family were in the same general area. They all faced the water as the castle was situated on its edge. According to the historical texts, one of the priests had deemed this the spot most connected to the gods and proclaimed it the best place to make the heart of the kingdom. The priest had blessed the place, but those blessings had been taken for granted.

Audra took a deep breath, readying herself for the conversation to come. With a sigh, she pushed open the door. "Ah," her father drawled. Even though he seemed composed, Audra could hear the anger behind his words. "You're here. Have a seat. And, close the door behind you."

Audra did as she was told. The office was the same gray stone as the rest of the castle, with an ornate wooden desk in the middle of the room. Her father sat in a red leather chair with gold accents. The chair Audra sat on was the same red leather but with silver accents. The two walls on either side of her were covered in bookshelves that held battle plans and tax sheets. Behind her father was a large window with the same arched top as most of the others in the palace.

Her father was an old man. His hair, which used to be a

dark brown, was now turning white. Wrinkles had yet to take over his face, but they were still there. His face was permanently set in a scowl. He had a tan complexion from the sun. As a king, he always wore fancy clothes of eed fabrics and animal pelts. A gold crown was always present on his head.

As Audra sat down, he finally started talking. "Do you know why you're here?"

"No. I was hoping you would tell me," she sassed, regretting it almost immediately.

She could see a vein on her father's head bulge in anger. "Earlier today a siren was spotted at the docks. Witnesses say you interacted with it."

Audra froze. *That idiot got caught!? At least she's not dead. But she might have made me be.* She fumed. Surprisingly, it wasn't really anger that she felt. No, it was concern. She'd deal with that thought later though, as right now she had a very angry father to diffuse. "They must have mistaken it for another person. I did run into someone, yes, but they weren't a siren," she assured him calmly, though that calm was fake.

He didn't look impressed. But, thankfully, he dropped the subject. That was the fastest she had ever seen him drop something. Audra had definitely gotten better at lying over the years. "There is one more thing I would like to discuss with you."

Ah, Audra thought. *That's why he dropped it so quickly. I'm not going to like this, am I?*

The king picked up some papers that were on his desk, straightening them while he talked. A sign he didn't think what they were talking about was serious. "A few months ago

I sent word to the kingdoms of Grenoria, Cerulean, and Aureolin. Tomorrow, the princes of those kingdoms will arrive and start to court you. At the end of the month, I expect you to choose one of them to marry."

Audra's mouth dropped open in shock. "What!? You can't be serious!" she yelled.

Her father's face hardened. "We could be attacked at any minute. If something should happen to me during the war, there will be no king to lead this country and keep it standing."

At this point, Audra was fuming. Yes, she knew the topic of marriage would eventually come up, but not now! She knew war was on the horizon. When you decide to commit mass genocide, you're going to make many enemies. Especially if the people you decide to kill are sirens. Sirens are known to be vengeful. If one of them is hurt they will go after whoever hurt them and will not stop until that person is destroyed. That's why the wall was built in the first place. It wasn't to keep people in, it was to keep other sirens out. Without it, they would tear the small island kingdom to pieces. To make matters worse, many siren pods had an excellent relationship with the kingdoms they shared waters with. They would be more than willing to help out their siren allies.

Audra hadn't been allowed to hear the speech her father had made when the murders started, but she knew it was bad based on what she heard from the few knights she was friends with. He had basically said they were stronger than the forces of the rest of the world combined. Rightfully, the knights had freaked out at that. But they were scared of her father and didn't have the guts to up and leave. So, they followed orders and did as they were told. The entire thing seemed to leave a bad taste in the knights' mouths.

Audra had talked to them about this when she went to train with them. Her father knew, but he never let her do any knight activities like tournaments or ceremonies. He also wouldn't knight her because in his eyes, knights were only men. Audra thought that was stupid.

"I'm not marrying some random prince!" she yelled. "I can take care of this kingdom on my own. I know it better than some prince from another kingdom ever could!"

"What will you do in a battle!?" her father yelled back. "The knights won't follow your command. A king must be here so someone can lead the troops!"

"I can lead the troops! You've seen me fight. You can't deny that I'm good. I've studied battle strategies for years!"

"Studying does not compare to actual battle experience, which you have none of."

Audra sunk down in her chair, crossing her arms. "Yeah, and who's fault is that?" she mumbled.

Her father banged his hand down on the table, making her jump in her seat. "That is quite enough young lady. Have you forgotten the deal we made?" That shut her up. He was talking about removing her from the line of succession again. "You will marry one of the princes whether you like it or not. And that is final."

Audra glared and stomped out of the room. She needed to cool off, and she sure as the gods couldn't do it here. Without much thought, only rage, she stormed to the stables. Servants moved out of her way when they saw her pass. One of the serving boys alerted the stable hand of the princess's current mood, and he was waiting for her with her horse ready to go when she arrived.

She smiled at him. "Thank you," she said, running her hand through the mane of her horse, a brown mare with a black mane and tail she had named Victory. She didn't mean to take her anger out on the castle staff. They weren't the ones doing anything wrong. The stable hand nodded silently and made his way back inside.

With practiced ease, Audra mounted her horse. She turned towards the water, admiring its beauty in the sunset. With a "Hua!" she was off into the trees near the beach.

Chapter 3

"Well," Audra said to her horse. "We are definitely lost." Her horse neighed, probably not in response, but Audra decided to think it was. The sun had gone down about three hours ago if she had to guess, and she was, at this point, stumbling blindly through the forest. And talking to a horse.

At least it was a nice forest. All forests in Carnelian were nice, but the ones behind the castle were some of her favorites. It was all due to nostalgia, as she and her mother used to go for rides through the forest. The trees were a mix of evergreen trees with thin branches and spiky, needle-like leaves, and massive old-growth trees. They had grown on the island for longer than there had been a kingdom here, and it showed in their size and the thick moss that grew over them. She was off the beaten path now, which meant she did have to keep her eyes out for blackberry bushes. She didn't have to worry about stinging nettle or poison ivy because she had tall boots and pants, but her horse did so she still kept her eyes peeled.

She groaned and tilted her head back before

dismounting. "We're not getting home tonight, are we?" she asked, once again talking to her horse as she tied his reigns to one of the evergreen trees. She sighed, laying down on the damp forest floor. It was cold, but there wasn't really anywhere else to sleep. At least it was mossy and not rock-hard.

Through the evergreen tree branches, Audra could see the stars. She could recognize a few constellations but had never taken the time to learn them. She did know the stories though. The stars were created as a way for the gods to view the world. Little eyes to see everything. It's said that if you ask something of the stars one of the gods will respond.

Audra sighed. "I can't believe I'm doing this," she mumbled. Picking a random star in the sky, she started speaking to it. "I want someone to talk to," she said. "I want to have a conversation with someone that isn't a horse."

She wasn't expecting anything to happen, but then she could hear a noise she hadn't heard before. It sounded like a voice. A girl's voice, If Audra had to guess. High in pitch. She wasn't singing any words Audra recognized but it was beautiful nonetheless. One of the most beautiful things she'd ever heard, honestly. It was faint like it was coming from some far-off place. So, with nothing to lose other than time, she decided to follow it.

Eventually, Audra reached a rock face. It wasn't huge, but it was large enough that most people would just go around it if they came across it. Audra wasn't most people. The voice was coming from the other side of the rock, and by the gods, it sounded beautiful. Seeing who it belonged to wasn't a want anymore, it was a need. She felt enchanted like someone had taken her brain and flown away with it. Maybe, in other circumstances, she would have realized what was happening. But she didn't. It took a bit of doing, but eventually, she was able to climb one of the smaller trees and vault onto the top of the ledge. Probably not her greatest decision but hey! It worked.

The ledge wasn't as big as she had anticipated. She could probably lay down flat across it with not much room to spare. The ledge itself went around in a circular shape, surrounding a drop-off. Curious, Audra moved closer to the cliff. She gasped in shock at what she saw.

It was a grotto. A beautiful lake surrounded by large rock formations. The water itself was dark and deep. Audra couldn't see the bottom. It would be dark in the grotto if it wasn't for the bioluminescent moss that hung from the top of the ledge Audra was standing on. The green, pink, and blue glow gave the entire place a majestic air. It didn't feel human. It felt like where some kind of deity would dwell.

As for where the music was coming from? Well, sitting on a rock a little way to Audra's left was the siren from the market. *Her?!* Audra screamed internally. *Great. I come out here to try and stop thinking about her and then run into her anyway. Just my luck.*

Audra looked at the girl again, taking in all of her appearance. She was white with a light tan. Her skin was clear, unlike Audra's which was covered in freckles. Her face was round, framed nicely by a cascade of flowing blonde hair. This time, Audra could see her tail. She had seen sirens' tails before, but she hadn't ever had the time to properly take in their beauty. The scales were metallic and shiny, with nice alternating emerald green and dark blue colors. Her fin looked like fine glass and was spread over rods of colored metal, shades of blues and greens.

She was, Audra admitted, very attractive. She had come to the realization a few years ago that her attraction went both ways. She found men attractive but at the same time also found women attractive. She had been fourteen at the time. At first, she had assumed it was just a phase, but it's now been three years and she's realized being attracted to both men and women was just part of who she was.

Audra crawled forward a bit, wanting to get a better look at the amazingly beautiful girl in front of her. She was so enchanted she didn't realize how thin the ledge was.

Crash! The rock broke, sending Audra tumbling into the cold waters. She couldn't breathe. It was dark, so dark she couldn't see her own hands. The saltwater stung her eyes. She tried to swim only to get her feet tangled in the moss she had taken down with her. She didn't even have time to think of any last words. Her mind just running a constant loop of *fear fear fear.*

And then there was light. Blinding and light blue. A figure came toward her, and just as she was about to fall into unconsciousness there was a foreign feeling on her lips. Hesitantly, Audra opened her eyes. Only to be met by the most beautiful eyes she had ever seen. Emerald green pupils that looked like gems surrounded by a sea of dark blue where the whites should be. The siren's eyes. Audra, the princess of

Carnelian, was being kissed by a siren. And she couldn't deny that she kind of liked it.

The kiss was broken all too quickly when the siren raised her hand and a bubble of blue magic surrounded them, allowing Audra to breathe. The siren smiled as she grabbed Audra around the waist and pulled the two of them up onto the rock she was previously sitting on. Her hold was gentle but strong.

Audra collapsed onto her hands and vomited. It wasn't the impression she had wanted to make on the cute siren girl but it had to happen. She had to get all that water out somehow. It was made up for when she felt a hand on her back rubbing comforting circles. "There, there," the siren soothed.

When Audra was done with her vomiting fest, she rolled over and put her hands over her eyes. The siren did some magic with her hand and used the water to clean up the mess. "I'm sorry," Audra mumbled.

The siren smiled. "No need to be sorry. Everyone has to vomit sometimes. Would have happened sooner or later." She stuck out a hand as Audra sat up, and she admired how the patches of scales around her wrists looked like gauntlets. "I'm Hali. And you seem to have fallen for me," she joked.

Audra laughed a weak laugh and took her hand, pulling herself up into a sitting position so the two were facing each other. "If my memory serves me right, you fell for me first."

Hali flushed and crossed her arms over her chest. "That's irrelevant."

Audra smiled. "Was that your attempt at flirting with me?"

Hali flushed even more. "Maybe..." she mumbled.

"It was cheesy."

Hali glared. "Hey! I think it was good."

At that Audra full-on laughed. She really wasn't all that intimidated, and her anger was actually kind of cute. Hali cracked a smile and was soon giggling next to her. After their giggling faded out, the two simply sat in comfortable silence.

"Why did you let me go?" Hali asked in a whisper. It was almost so quiet that Audra couldn't hear her.

"What was that?" she asked.

"Why did you let me go? You're supposed to hate me. Your father does." Hali explained weakly, fiddling with her hands.

Audra felt her temper flare. "*I am not my father!*" she yelled, immediately regretting it when Hali flinched back violently. "I'm sorry..." she tried again. "I shouldn't have yelled. I just hate it when people compare me to *him*," she explained, spitting the last word out like vile. "I don't share my father's views. I was primarily raised by my mother, and she taught me that we should protect every citizen. No matter if they're human or siren."

Hali smiled. "Your mother sounds like a lovely woman."

Audra looked down. "She was."

"Was?"

"She's gone."

Hali stilled. "Oh..." she eventually said. The two sat in

silence again. This one was not as peaceful as before. Hali grabbed Audra's hand after a minute. "Mine too," she mumbled.

Audra inwardly winced at that. She knew the most likely reason why. "I'm sorry for your loss." That was all she could say, as lame as it was. She knew that wouldn't help the pain, but she didn't know what else to say.

Hali smiled again. "So, why are you out here?" she asked, effectively ending their earlier conversation. Audra wasn't inclined to restart it, anyway.

"I got in a fight with my father." She shrugged. "Nothing too major. Actually..." She grabbed Hali by the shoulders and shook her. Hali flopped like even more of a fish. "You idiot! Did you seriously get caught!? See! I told you it was dangerous!"

She stopped shaking Hali. "I know it's dangerous," Hali grumbled. "And I was being careful! Things just happened to go wrong."

"Well, you could have been more careful."

"Please, do enlighten me, how?"

Audra rolled her eyes. "Oh, I don't know. Maybe not taking one of the main paths?"

That made Hali pause. "While I will admit that would have probably been a better option," Audra smirked. "I will counter with I don't know my way around."

Audra's smirk dropped. "That does make sense."

Now Hali smirked. "*Ha!*" She pumped her fist in the air.

Again, an easy silence came over the two. Audra took

a minute to take in where they were. From the angle they were at, the grotto looked a whole different kind of beautiful. The glowing moss mixed with the night sky and stars. The water, while still deep, now had a reflection of the stars.

"This place is sacred among the sirens," Hali started. "It's known as Lover's Grotto. The water is incredibly deep, and while you can't see it from here the outside walls have been intricately carved by our craftsmen. This place is only ever used for ceremonies. Weddings, name givings," Hali paused, her words seemingly stuck in her throat. "And funerals."

Audra nodded. "I can see why. It's absolutely breathtaking."

Hali smiled. "I'm glad you think so. To my knowledge, you're the first human to see it."

Audra was shocked. "I'm not supposed to be here, am I?" she eventually asked.

Hali shook her head. "Not really, no. But, for some reason, I feel like you're meant to be here."

"I found this place because I asked the gods for someone I could talk to. Then I heard you when I hadn't before and followed the sound here."

"Why would you follow an unknown voice through the forest? I don't know much about forests," she gestured to her tail, "for pretty obvious reasons, but if they're anything like kelp forests following random voices sounds like a bad idea."

Audra blanked. "Actually, that's a good question. That isn't something I would normally do."

"Wait." Hali froze. "Did I accidentally enchant you? Oh no, I accidentally enchanted you! I'm sorry!"

"Calm down!" She laughed. "I'm not mad! I'm glad you did, truthfully."

"Why?"

"Because if you didn't, I wouldn't have met you."

"Oh. Well, then I have to agree. You're a lovely person to have met. Properly this time," Hali told her.

Audra smiled. "Right. Besides, at least now I can say you're enchanting."

"Oh shut up!"

CHAPTER 4

I was wondering," Audra asked. "What did you do earlier, with the light? Was that siren magic?"

Hali smiled at the other girl. Really, she wasn't exactly sure how she ended up in this situation. She came to the grotto to relax and then all of a sudden she was kissing the (actually very hot) princess. And to think, only a little while ago she had been scared this lovely woman was going to kill her.

"Yep! That was a tiny bit of siren magic. Relatively basic stuff. I'm not very good at magic," she answered.

"Really? It looked pretty powerful to me," Audra said.

Hali blushed. "It's not. Creating light is one of the easiest things to do. Everyone uses it to light up their houses. Well, they used to at least."

Audra retracted her arm, and Hali found she already missed the warmth her embrace gave. "So what else can you do?" she questioned.

Hali lit up. "Well, some people can create things out of water. Things created like that usually are clear. Sometimes objects made like that can show images. I can do that, but more advanced stuff like any shape other than a sphere or any other spell is out of my league. Also, people can move water at will. That's pretty versatile and people have figured out how to do a lot of different things with that."

"I can imagine." Audra smiled, very obviously impressed. Hali felt weirdly proud of being able to impress her.

"The most famous magic people know about is our song magic. It's kind of like mind control so we can eat people's souls. We have to sing about a person's inner desire. Usually, that's sex, but occasionally it's not. And about the whole eating souls thing, I honestly wouldn't do it if I didn't need to survive. And most sirens only have to eat a soul six times a year, so every two months. Oh! And then there's my favorite part! I can change my gender at will!"

Audra's eyebrows shot up. "Really?"

Hali nodded, beaming. "Yes really! It's super cool! A lot of people only use this ability during feeding, but I personally like to use it whenever I want to. I don't like being a girl all the time, you know?" Audra nodded while smiling, and Hali beamed even more. "Would you like to see what I look like when I'm a boy?" she asked.

"I would love to. Please," Audra answered.

Hali smiled and felt her magic connect to the water. His breasts shrank under the silk tank top he was wearing. He felt his hair shrink as well, becoming a messy cut that fell just below his ears. His features became a little bit more defined, and when he spoke his voice was lower in pitch, but still relatively high. "See!"

Audra smiled and pulled him into a hug. "You're adorable," she mumbled.

They talked for hours about nothing. Or maybe about everything, the difference was hard to tell when having a good conversation. Either way, the moon was high in the sky by the time they started to wrap up.

"I need—" Audra yawned. "I need to head back."

"You're leaving?" Hali mumbled. He had curled up against Audra's chest and found it was quite a comfortable spot.

"I have a big day tomorrow. I need to sleep." She gently rolled him off of her and into the water. He dived under for a minute, letting the water's power wake him up. Audra stood up and looked at the ledge. "I don't actually know how I'm supposed to leave."

"I can lift you over to the other side," Hali said as he fully got out of the water. His tail shifted to legs, and once again he was stumbling forward. Audra caught him before he could fall, so it was worth it. "And I've fallen for you again. It's becoming a problem at this point."

"Are you seriously going to keep making that joke?"

"Yes. Every time."

She laughed. "Hali, you're a wonder."

Hali blushed. "Audra?" he asked.

"Yes?"

"Will I ever see you again?"

Audra's smile turned sad. "Hali…"

"Please," he begged. "I don't want to be

alone anymore."

"It's dangerous," Audra reminded him. "I wish it wasn't but it is."

"I know that."

"Especially if I come to see you. I could be followed from the palace. It's too much of a risk—"

"I want to risk it!" he interrupted. "For you, I want to risk it."

"For me?"

He fidgeted. "And maybe a little for myself."

Audra's eyes warmed. She reached up and patted his shoulder. "Then I will come back."

Hali beamed. "Tomorrow?"

"Tomorrow. Until then..." Audra trailed off and looked at the top of the ledge. "Be safe, Hali."

Waking up the next morning wasn't something Hali wanted to do. The last night had been so magical, it could have been a dream. Either way, Hali wished he could spend the day laying on his soft kelp bed. But the ocean had other plans for him, it seemed.

Hali shot up in bed. His chest felt tight. It wasn't an emotion, it was magic. Specifically, it was the kind of passive magic felt when other sirens were near. He grabbed his satchel in a flash and swam out the window. There were other sirens around, and he was going to find them.

Sirens relied on having other sirens around. They hunted in pods, built homes in pods, and lived in pods. Siren magic was stronger when there were more of them. So naturally, being without other sirens for a few months had taken a toll on Hali. He was lonely. That might have been why he latched onto Audra so quickly. While she didn't have siren magic, she herself was magical. Not in the literal sense, of course. Hali just felt like she was.

He swam through the abandoned city that used to be home to the Evergreen Pod. A place that used to be bright and full of life was now dull and empty. The whole place was built with intricately carved rock. Sconces held clear orbs that used to be lights but had long since gone dark when the person keeping them lit passed on. Hali had summoned his own light orb, as the water was naturally dark and it was hard to see. The blue light cast a strange, eerie glow on the walls. Most were covered in art. Mosaics, carvings, and murals depict moments in the pod's history, both good and bad. They had all been handmade by artisans throughout the years. Hali's own mother had made quite a few of the more recent ones, even having the honor to sculpt King Milos when he had first come into power.

Now, it hurt to see those designs. He didn't stay in the city for long. He swam through quickly.

Past the city was a rocky field on the sea floor. It had been a farm once. The moss and kelp that grew on the rocks had been carefully cultivated and collected. No one was here to collect it anymore, but Hali still liked to stop by and pick bits of it every once in a while. Past that was the sand field, his destination. A long sandy stretch of land that had been carefully cleared of all rocks. Spread along the edge were small rock huts that held sporting equipment for the pod to use.

There wasn't space to play on the field anymore, as cutting directly through the field was the wall. It was an imposing structure. Tall, iron bars stretched all the way down from the top of the water to the ocean floor. Hali could see through them, but try as he might he couldn't fit anything more than his arm through. Every few miles, towers of stone rose from the sea, all of them connected by a stone walkway on top of the bars. Guards were posted at each tower, with orders to harpoon any siren who got too close. The only way in was through a swinging gate that was heavily guarded. There was no way Hali could make it through.

There, on the other side, illuminated by their glowing orbs, was a group of sirens. About fifteen in total. One of them, an elderly siren in the middle, was the first to notice him. "Child?" they asked.

Hali held back a sob as he took in their appearance. They were old and had ocher brown skin. Their long white hair was pulled into a ponytail behind a crown of gold. Their scales looked as if they were made of gold and copper, signifying them as a member of some royal household. They wore a golden chest plate and held a magnificent gold trident. Their eyes were kind and were the colors of honey and silver.

"You're here," Hali eventually said. Hot, slimy purple tears spilled over despite him trying to hold them back. "You actually came."

The ruler smiled sadly. "Oh, little one. Of course, we would come. Sirens protect their kind. And if they can't, they avenge them. I'm just sorry it took us so long to get here."

Hali did sob at that. He leaned against the bars of the gate and felt the muscled arms of the other siren wrap around him as much as they could. He let himself cry, not holding anything in. He cried, for what seemed like, and probably was, hours. Hali hadn't cried since Marni had passed on, leaving him alone. He should have let himself. But instead, he bottled up all those terrible feelings and let them fall the minute he felt even the slightest bit of sympathy.

Eventually, when he had shed all the tears he could, he looked back up at the ruler. "I'm sorry…" he mumbled after he very suddenly remembered that he had just cried his eyes out in front of a member of the siren royalty.

The royal only smiled. "It's quite alright. My name is Ruler Athos. I am the ruler of the Shining Sea Pod." They gestured behind them to the other sirens. "And this is my royal guard."

Hali nodded. "My name is Hali. Thank you for coming," he answered, trying to be at least somewhat formal.

"Are there others with you?" Ruler Athos asked.

"No. It's just me," he replied, shaking his head.

The ruler's expression turned grim. "Well, it's better than what we thought. With the amount of despair energy coming from this place we had thought there would be no one left."

Hali grimaced. "Well, one is better than zero, at least." He tried to joke, laughing awkwardly at the end.

The ruler grimaced. "Yes, it is. Are you safe where you are staying currently?" Hali nodded. He wasn't exactly going to admit his stupid mistake in getting caught, now was he?

"Good. We have a plan in place. We have an ally we will be meeting on land. They have already infiltrated the kingdom. When we get the signal, our forces will attack the wall and bring it down. I recommend being away from the wall when that happens. We will find you after the battle is through."

Hali nodded. The ruler was authoritative and he could tell this plan had been set in stone long before he had even been in the picture. Then it hit him. *What will they do to Audra? If I didn't know she was good then they definitely don't.*

"What will happen to the princess?" he asked.

The ruler looked momentarily surprised but hid it quickly. "She was a part of this massacre so she shall be killed along with her father."

"*You can't do that!*" Hali yelled before he could think. He just yelled at a royal. Not the best move on his part. *But,* he thought, *this is for Audra. Nobody hurts Audra. Not on my watch.*

"I'm sorry?" Ruler Athos asked, reasonably confused.

"I said, you can't do that. Audra is a good person. She doesn't share her father's ideals. I think she'll be a wonderful queen," Hali said.

He squared his shoulders and tried to look as intimidating as possible. In the words of Hali's best friend Marni "You only get scary when you're truly furious, and usually, then you're not even trying. When you actually try and look scary you just look like a blown-up pufferfish."

Ruler Athos did seem to see Hali's determination, though, because they looked somewhat confused. "That is very interesting. I was not aware she didn't support her father. I will relay this information to our ally."

Hali deflated. "Good." He smiled.

The Ruler smiled lightly. "You speak as if you know her. May I ask how?"

Hali thought for a second before nodding. "She's my friend."

The young siren swam home, and Ruler Athos dropped their smile as soon as he was out of sight. So did the rest of their troops. "At ease, soldiers." They breathed out, letting the soldiers mutter to each other.

"Poor kid..." the general, their second in command, whispered. She had white skin and chestnut brown hair, which was pulled neatly into a bun on her head. Her orange and silver scales glowed in the cold water. Her armor was scuffed from years of use, but it still fit her like a glove.

Athos nodded. "That child has gone through something terrible."

"What can we do?" she asked.

"Support them. Offer a space for them to be safe once all of this is over," they answered.

"And when will that be?" the general pressed on. "This changes things."

"And what does it change?" Athos countered. The general paused. She didn't have an answer. "It's a slight adjustment, sure. But one we can make."

She glared at the wall. It was an ugly sight. Sections of bars with towers every mile, plunging through the waves and into the rocks and sand below. Athos wondered how it was built. It must not have been easy. Humans were inventive builders, but for them to have built something of this scale so quickly? Athos was skeptical, to say the least. It looked impossible. But, then again. All the evilest things seem that way.

"I want to kill them," the general eventually said, her eyes still fixed on the only thing keeping them from charging in. "The whole kingdom. Even the princess."

"I understand your anger," Athos soothed.

"Then why don't you act on it!?" she snapped.

"Because it is not my anger to feel. It's his," Athos explained. "We are here to offer support to the fallen. Had there been no Evergreen Sea Pod to meet us, we would have been able to go on the rampage you wish for. However, he was here. And he told us what his wishes were. For us not to hurt Princess Audra. We are in his waters. We must respect his wishes."

The general didn't say anything, she merely shifted her gaze to the sea floor.

Athos sighed. "Besides, the child has been through enough losses already. His grief should not be on our hands."

She turned to look at them. "I suppose you are right. I'm sorry my anger got the best of me."

"It's alright, friend. It happens to all of us." Athos turned to the troops. "Everyone. We are to head back to our camp. I must consult with our ally." As the troops filed away, Athos took one last look through the gates and into the dark waters on the other side. "Child," they prayed, "be smart. And be safe."

Chapter 5

udra very much didn't want to get out of bed when she woke up the morning after meeting Hali. She knew what was coming when she went downstairs. Boys would try and flirt with her. It was going to be exhausting. *The only boy I want flirting with me is Hali,* she thought.

Her daydreams about her new siren friend (Were they friends? She would hope so.) were interrupted by a knock on her door. "Milady? May I come in?" Lila's very identifiable voice rang out.

Audra smiled. Lila always had a way of bringing up her mood. "Come in!" she called.

Lila waltzed in, looking very pleased with whatever she was thinking about. "Oh princess, you're in for a treat today. I was just talkin' to some of the other maids, and they say the princes that arrived last evening are very dashing."

Audra smiled. "I'm glad the maids are enjoying themselves."

Lila eyed her up and down. "Well, I'm not sure why you're not so excited about this, darlin'. If I had three strapping young gentlemen fallin' over themselves to woo me I'd be happy as a sunflower!"

Audra didn't exactly know what that meant, and she seriously doubted she ever would. But that was just Lila being Lila. She rolled her eyes. "I don't want other boys trying to woo me," she grumbled.

Lila's eyes widened. "Are you saying there is someone?" That made Audra blush and look down at the ground. Lila laughed. "Oh deary me! That's certainly a shocker. So, who's the lucky guy or gal?"

Audra, still looking at the floor, sighed. "You don't know them."

"I know a lot of people, honey. Try me."

Audra smiled. "You definitely don't. And as much as I trust you, it's safer for him if people don't know who he is."

She stood up and walked behind the changing screen in the corner. Her room was rectangular. On one of the long walls, there was a glass door that led out onto a balcony facing the ocean. The rest of the wall was covered in square windows that filled the room with natural light. The door was on the opposite wall. A large cedar table sat in the middle of the room, a few chairs surrounding it. On the left side of the room was Audra's bed. A red silk canopy covered the top. In the corner on the door side was a cedar changing screen and a vanity. A dresser was on the wall near the door. On the opposite wall was a fireplace with two swords and a shield hanging above.

Lila smiled as she handed Audra the dress she had picked out for her. Usually, Audra picked out her own clothes, but today was a special occasion. Lila knew the best way to make an impression, and she trusted Lila's judgment on formal wear much more than her own. "Well, I'm glad you found someone. I hope they make you happy."

"Lila, he somehow makes me feel both wonderful and terrible at the same time. Like I'm on top of the world but at any minute it all could crumble and I'll be back at the bottom. It's strange, but I kind of like it," she explained from behind the screen. After a minute, she came out. Lila had picked out a long, flowing red dress with a low-cut bodice and long sleeves with open shoulders.

"Well, that sounds lovely, honey. I can tell you are dyin' to rant about him. Tell me more," Lila prodded as she started putting Audra's brown hair into a bun.

Audra smiled dreamily. "Lila, he's wonderful. He's funny, caring, and he's so cheesy." She deflated a bit. "But he probably doesn't even like me like that. I mean, he has plenty of reasons not to."

"Don't talk like that!" Lila glared. "You are a wonderful person. I can't see a reason why anyone in their right mind wouldn't want to have you." She smiled, and Audra looked at herself in the mirror. "And there you are. Pretty as a peach."

Audra smiled. "Thank you, Lila," she whispered.

Lila smiled softly. "It's my honor." She looked Audra in the eyes. "You're going to make a great queen, darlin'. The people already love you. You don't need a king for them to follow you. Remember that."

"I will," Audra answered. And with that, she turned

and walked out to go face her new suitors.

She took a deep breath and pushed open the door to the main dining hall. "Ah!" Her father's voice sounded out, ringing through the hall like thunder. "Here's my wonderful daughter! Audra! Have a seat."

Audra had to resist the urge to roll her eyes. When her father was trying to impress visiting nobles he'd put on this fake act of being all sweet to make it seem like they were close. As much as she hated it, there wasn't much she could do except go along. As much as she didn't like it, she could understand the strategy behind it. Having a family divided was an obvious weakness that could be exploited by others. "Hello, Father," she answered, begrudgingly pretending to be excited. She took a seat in one of the red and gold chairs.

"Boys," the king began, "I would like to introduce you to Princess Audra of Carnelian." Audra nodded as she was supposed to. "Audra, I would like to introduce you to Prince Ajax of Grenoria, Prince Mel of Cerulean, and Prince Cassius of Aureolin."

Audra took a moment to take in all three boys. Prince Ajax sat on her left. He was a tall, muscular blonde who was sitting with an air of confidence. *No,* she thought. *Not confidence. Arrogance.* He had a smirk on his face and was looking around as if he would soon own the place. He wore armor with a long green cape with his family's crest on the back, not something one would usually consider wearing to breakfast. Audra was not at all surprised to see that he had a sword at his side. Audra could see why some would find him attractive, but personally, he seemed like a brute to her.

Prince Cassius sat across from her. He had black skin with cold hazel eyes and hair cut close to his head. He wore an intricately stitched yellow coat with matching yellow pants and boots. Even from across the table, Audra could see how the threading shined, indicating it was made of gold. A subtle display of Aureolins' staggering wealth. Cassius was well collected, with a perfect poker face gained from growing up as a royal. If Audra had to pick out of all three princes, she would have to say Cassius was the most attractive one. *Not as attractive as Hali though.*

Compared to Prince Cassius, Prince Mel looked like a walking disaster. He was a small, pale boy with a mop of curly bright orange hair and a massive amount of freckles. He had on a plain light blue tunic with flowy sleeves and a blue vest, dark blue pants, and black leather boots. He looked so nervous that Audra almost found it amusing. His round eyes darted wildly from Ajax to the king and then to her. She could understand why. He had not been a prince for long. The island where Cerulean is now was once a colony of Grenoria, which along with Aureolin was located on the mainland. They had only won their revolution three years ago, and from what Audra knew, Mel's parents had been war generals.

All three of them had a reason to be here and it wasn't romance. For Mel and Ajax, that reason was easy to determine. Grenoria was one of the only kingdoms to remain allies with Carnelian after the purge started. They had offered support when the killing first started. Ajax was here as both insurance that the kingdoms would remain allies and try to secure the valuable trade routes that Carnelian had. Mel's kingdom was still scrambling after the war. They needed allies right about now and were desperate enough to send their new and only prince to a different kingdom to try and secure an alliance.

Cassius's reasons for being here, on the other hand, were a complete mystery. Logically speaking, there was absolutely nothing to gain from an alliance with Carnelian. They had trade routes through their alliance with Cerulean. Already they were the wealthiest kingdom in the world, and they also had one of the largest armies. So really, Cassius's motivation for coming here was a mystery, one Audra was kind of excited to figure out.

While Audra pondered on this, someone had come in with breakfast. The table was laid out with heaps of meat, eggs, fruit, and pastries. A meal fit for royalty, literally. One of the cooks took his place next to the king, head held high. "Your Highnesses," he greeted.

"Hello." Mel smiled. Ajax sent him a glare, causing him to retreat back into his shell and sink deeper into his seat. Audra and Cassius nodded respectfully, while Ajax merely grunted at the cook and the king chose to completely ignore his presence altogether.

The cook smiled at Mel and continued with his speech. "Breakfast is served." And with that, his role was over. He bowed lightly and retreated back to the kitchens.

Ajax was the first to dig into the food, heaping his plate high with meat and eggs. Audra scoffed when he reached over her to get to it. Everyone else grabbed much less, and unlike Ajax, actually asked for others to pass things they couldn't reach.

"So," the king started, "Ajax. I've heard you've recently had some success in battle."

Everyone who was not Ajax and the king froze. The king was talking about the Cerulean independence war. *What in the world is he thinking!? I thought this was a diplomatic endeavor. How is provoking one of the princes diplomatic?!* she screamed in her mind.

"Why yes, I have, your highness! I've won quite a few battles in my years leading the troops." Ajax bragged, sending a smirk to Mel. "My men and I were on Cerulean, trying to keep the peasants in line, you understand. The rebels thought they were so clever. They had placed their base in the woods, thinking that would keep them safe. They were so easy to find, and soon enough we had them surrounded."

Mel tensed. His eyes widened and his breathing picked up. *He was there.* Audra realized.

"Ajax. That's quite enough," Cassius interrupted, beating her to put a stop to this.

He only laughed. "Don't be such a girl, Cass." Cassius bristled at the nickname. "What? Can't handle a joke? So, back to what I was saying. It was nighttime when my men stormed in. We took out their door guards before they could even call for help. They screamed like little babies, it was quite amusing."

"Prince Ajax. You are being incredibly rude. Change the subject. Now," Audra demanded.

Ajax ignored her. "They weren't prepared. We swarmed them easily, They didn't even stand a—"

Mel slammed his hand on the table, standing up with a dark look in his eyes. "Excuse me," he said, quickly walking out of the room. Cassius looked worried for a minute but quickly masked it. He stood up, nodding politely at the other three people in the room before turning and swiftly following Mel.

"Well, now I guess it's just us," Ajax said, looking at Audra in a way that made her extremely uncomfortable.

Audra stood up, glaring daggers at the two men in the room. "That was the most immature display I have ever seen from men of your standing. And I have seen some very immature things," Audra stated, her voice cold with a tinge of underlying fury. Both men tried to keep their composure, but Audra could see the small hints that told her they were scared. *Good. They should be.* "I'll be taking my leave now. You finish your meal. I want you to think long and hard about what you just did. Good day." And with that, she turned on her heel and stormed out of the room, her dress flowing behind her in a cool way that makes her feel unexplainably powerful.

Mel and Cassius weren't hard to find. She could hear loud sobs coming from an unused room a little way down the hall. She could hear Cassius's silky voice trying to comfort the other boy. That wasn't something she was expecting him to be doing, but it wasn't a bad thing. He had seemed cool earlier and this only made him seem cooler. "It's Princess Audra, may I come in?"

There was a bit of muttering before Mel shakily responded, "Yes."

Audra opened the door slowly, closing it behind her.

She knew it would make the situation worse if someone were to walk in. It wasn't really about embarrassment and more about reputation, something that was important seeing as all three of them were royalty.

Mel was sitting on top of a chest Audra didn't even know the contents of. He was frantically trying to wipe tears off his face but it wasn't working because they were being replaced just as quickly as they came. Cassius was kneeling in front of him and he had a hand on Mel's knee comfortingly. "I came to apologize on behalf of my father and Prince Ajax's actions. What they did was deliberate and wrong. I'm sorry."

Mel laughed weakly. "Don't apologize. You didn't do anything wrong. I'm sorry that situation happened in the first place."

Cassius softened. "It wasn't your fault either."

"He's right, you know. What happened wasn't your fault. It was my father's." She couldn't help the bit of venom that seeped into that word. Luckily, Mel didn't notice it. Unluckily, Cassius did if the glance he sent her was anything to go by. "And Prince Ajax. They are the ones to blame for this."

Mel only nodded. "Thank you. You know, I was worried you'd be a brat when I was on the way here. I'm happy you're not."

Audra laughed. "Thanks. I'm happy you're not a brute. You too, Prince Cassius."

"I appreciate that." Cassius nodded.

Audra clasped her hands together and smiled. "Well. I'll take my leave now. Unless there's anything else you need?"

Cassius shook his head. "No. I think that's it."

"Actually," Mel interjected, "where are the gardens?"

Audra smiled. "Down the hall to your right. There should be a big glass door that leads into the courtyard."

Mel grinned. "Thanks."

The Carnelian gardens are nice, Mel admitted to himself. Not nearly as nice as the ones at home, though. The Carnelian gardens clearly were not shown as much attention and love as he showed his. Still, they served their purpose. He felt much more grounded with soil under his hands. The soil felt the same even in this new country. Wet, yet still dusty. It was calming, to have something similar.

Cassius walked up behind him. He hummed in acknowledgment but didn't look up. He couldn't handle eye contact at the moment. Cassius knew that. He set the platter of food and tea on the ground next to Mel and sat down so they were back to back. He always liked sitting like this, leaning against Cassius's strong frame. He was a muscular man, and Mel knew that if push came to shove Cassius would be able to protect him.

Not that he couldn't protect himself. He knew he could. But sometimes it felt good to know he wouldn't have to fight alone.

"Are you alright?" Cassius asked, his voice the soft tone he always and only used with Mel.

"Not really, but I am feeling better," Mel told him. Cassius nodded. He didn't want to say more about the subject. Nothing more needed to be said.

"Cassius?" he asked, still staring at the ground. Cassius

hummed in response. "Why are we here?"

He frowned. "What do you mean?"

Mel shrugged. "Neither of us is going to marry Audra. She seems nice, but neither of us is going to marry her. So then, why are we here?"

"Diplomacy. Neither of us has met the royals of Carnelian, and it's important to establish a good relationship with a vital trade kingdom." Cassius answered, and Mel's heart sank. He was hiding something.

"Don't lie to me."

"I don't want to upset you."

"You're upsetting me by not telling me," he told him. "Cass, please. I don't want to be here. Not with him. And you know that. You wouldn't have brought me here without a reason."

Cassius sighed and leaned further up against Mel's back. "If I tell you, you'll be mad."

"I won't."

"You will though. I know you, Mel, and you will be mad."

Mel laughed and grabbed some dirt, letting it fall between his hands. "Just tell me, Cass."

"Well," Cassius began, the word short in the way all his words were when he was stressed. "The original goal was to lead a revolution to kill both the king and the princess for the massacre of the Evergreen Sea Pod."

"Cassius!" Mel shouted. "That is not something you neglect to tell me! And what do you mean originally?!"

Cassius hung his head. "I'm reviewing the plan with

new information. Maybe killing Princess Audra isn't the best way to go."

"Good, because I am pretty against killing the nice princess so far." Mel groaned and grabbed another fistful of dirt. He threw it into the flower bed, and it made a satisfying sound as it hit the leaves. "Just, how were you going to go about doing that anyway."

"The Shining Sea Pod followed us here."

Mel hung his head. "Gods above. They did?"

Cassius nodded. "Yes. And I was going to find an already started revolution. Which I have done."

"We are not letting them kill Princess Audra either."

"They weren't going to."

"Good." Mel picked up another chunk of dirt and let it fall. "So…"

"So what?"

"What can I do to help?"

Cassius blinked in surprise. "You will? Mel, If you don't want to you don't have to."

"I want to," he told him. "I trust you, Cass. And I trust your decisions. So, tell me how I can help."

CHAPTER 6

L ila was a good girl. She didn't like to lie. But even she knew there were times when it was needed. Like now.

"Lila?" the king drawled. She gulped. He didn't sound pleased. "Where is my daughter?"

The king had found her while she was doing some laundry and politely minding her own business. She hadn't seen Audra since this morning and hadn't thought much of it. Now, she realized, it seemed her little princess had snuck out. And Dad was mad.

"She's out on a ride with Prince Cassius," she fibbed quickly. He seemed like a fine gentleman, and the king did want the two to socialize.

He looked her up and down, disbelieving. Lila tried her hardest to remember her breathing. It wasn't easy, with him staring at her like that. Like she was nothing more than a pig on a platter. But, eventually, he just sighed. "The two could have at least told me first," he mumbled, before stomping off.

Lila breathed a sigh of relief. *Well,* she thought, *I am glad that's over. Now, I should probably give a little warning to*

Prince Cassius.

The prince wasn't hard to find, he was right where she thought he would be. In his room, minding his own business. He was easy like that. No guesswork needed. Unlike Audra, who could be anywhere in this world.

"Hello. What do you need?" he asked when she entered the room.

"Could I ask a favor of you, my lord?" Lila curtsied as she entered, less out of respect and more out of caution. She didn't know Cassius, and while he seemed to be a nice gentleman, she couldn't entirely know if he was trustworthy.

Like the gentleman Lila thought he was, he nodded in acknowledgment. He didn't need to do that, but he did it anyway. Or maybe that was actually the respectful thing to do, and she was just too used to the constant disrespect from the king. Cassius spoke. "If it is within my power, I will try my best to fulfill it."

She smiled at him. "Could you tell the king you were out with Audra this mornin' on a ride? It'd be best if he didn't know where she truly is."

He thought for a moment. "Could you tell me where Audra currently is?"

She shook her head sadly. "No. I'm sorry, I can't."

Cassius sighed. "Alright," he said eventually. "I'll tell the king we were out on a ride. But, I want something from you in return."

Lila gulped. *A choice, then.* She didn't know him. And she didn't like owin' nobody favors. Favors were important. Things you keep close to your chest and don't give out unless absolutely necessary. She could refuse, go back on her ask, but she wouldn't. This was about Audra. "What would you want?" she asked nervously.

He smiled kindly. "I would just like to ask you some questions. Nothing difficult. I promise I won't keep you from your duties for too long."

Lila breathed a sigh of relief. *Questions. I can answer questions. That's easy,* she thought. Cassius gestured to an empty chair, prompting her to sit. She did. "All right, what questions do you have?"

"Princess Audra, what is she like? Really."

"Sweet," Lila told him. That was an easy one, he had told the truth. She could talk about Audra for days. But for now she would keep it brief. "Audra's a strong girl. And she's kind. She has a good head on her shoulders."

Cassius took this all in seriously. He seemed genuinely intrigued by her answers. "And what do you think about the king?" he asked.

Lila had been told from a young age that "if you don't have anything nice to say, don't say it." So, she kept her mouth shut.

Cassius nodded like that was a reasonable answer. "You don't like him."

"I don't hold a high opinion of him, no. It's just that he's the king is all."

"The king, you say?"

"Yes. The king of this kingdom."

"And Audra is?"

"My princess."

Cassius hummed. "I see…. That's all I would like to ask of you for now. Would it be alright for me to seek you out to ask more questions later?"

Lila nodded. "You may. I don't mind, dear."

His smile was nice, and Lila thought that if Audra didn't already have someone in mind he would make a very good husband. But that wasn't her decision to make, nor an opinion she needed to share. Still, she approved of him. He wouldn't be terrible to have around the castle. He had a knowing look in his eyes. It was endearing. "I feel like we will be talking again, dear lady," he told her. "I feel we have some goals that may align."

Hali swam around in circles, blushing like a maniac. He felt like those sirens who used to swoon over the warriors. Marni called them lovesick fools, even if they did like the attention they got from being a warrior themselves. Hali used to tease Marni for all the people blushing over them. Now, if Marni were still alive, they'd be the ones teasing Hali.

Hali had been thinking about Audra for most of the day. Mostly about why he was so willing to trust her. And the realization had sent him spiraling. He had an absolutely humongous crush on Princess Audra. After debating with himself for a while and coming to the conclusion that this was true, he proceeded to scream into his pillow for a solid hour.

Which leads to what he's doing now. Swimming in circles, trying not to scream, while waiting for Audra to arrive. He was getting any embarrassment and self-consciousness out early so he could flirt to the best of his ability when she actually showed up.

As he finally calmed down, he felt movement in the water. He looked up, seeing a familiar hand breaking through the blurry surface. It waved and Hali chuckled, waving back before poking his head out of the water. There, sitting next to the water, was the one and only Audra. Beautiful brown locks framed her small smile. Hali smiled back. "Are you an octopus? Because you octo-pi my thoughts," he said instead of a traditional greeting.

Audra let out a loud guffaw, a sound that made Hali smile even more. "Really? That's the best you could come up with?" she joked.

Hali rolled his eyes playfully. "Hey! I'm trying!" he exclaimed, climbing out of the water to sit on the edge.

Audra ruffled his hair. "I'm sure you are." She leaned back, getting more comfortable on the rock. "So," she asked. "How was your day?"

Hali faltered a bit. *Should I tell her about Ruler Athos and the Shining Sea Pod? I mean, I trust Audra but they don't... No. I won't tell her.* "Eh, it was normal. Boring, but normal. Much better now that you're here."

"Well, mine was great but It's amazing now that I'm talking to you," Audra said.

Hali raised an eyebrow. "Really? What's so special about today?"

"Well, three princes came," Audra explained. Hali's smile turned down a bit, and Audra quickly backtracked. "I don't like any of them if that's what you're thinking. Breakfast was interesting, to say the least. One of them is a jerk and I'm pretty sure the other two are seeing each other."

Hali laughed, any jealousy he had dissipating quickly. "That sounds like it would be awkward."

"It wasn't. Mainly, I was just angry at Prince Ajax. He's the one who's a jerk. Prince Mel and Prince Cassius were nice, though. I talked with them a bit. They seem like they'd be good friends. I bet you'll like them, you kind of remind me of Mel."

He sighed. "I'd love to meet them. They sound like good people. But I'll never be able to meet them."

Audra frowned. "Actually, now that I'm thinking about it, I don't think they'd do anything. Mel's kingdom doesn't have a siren pod near it, and Cassius's kingdom has a strong relationship with the siren pod in its waters. The Shining Sea Pod, if my memories are correct."

Hali froze. *Ruler Athos said they had an ally in Carnelian. Could it be Prince Cassius? Would Cassius hurt Audra?* He shook his head. *No. Ruler Athos said they'd tell their ally Audra's good.*

"Do you know them? The Shining Sea Pod?" Audra asked. She had noticed Hali freeze.

"Yeah, they're super famous for being rich," he lied quickly, stuttering a little on his words. He'd never liked lying.

Audra noticed his lie but didn't pry, luckily. "Right. That makes sense because Aureolin is also famous for being the wealthiest kingdom in the world. Anyway, I think it wouldn't be too dangerous for you to meet them. If you're okay with it, of course."

Hali thought for a second, mulling it over. He was lonely and meeting Audra's friends wouldn't be half bad.

Despite the risk, he found himself wanting to agree. "Maybe. But you should get closer to them first. I'm not risking my life on people you only met today."

"That's acceptable." Audra nodded. "But, aren't you doing that right now? I mean, we only met yesterday."

"That's because you're different," he answered.

Audra gave him a confused look. "How?"

Hali stuttered. He couldn't really come up with an answer for that. So he just crossed his arms and turned his back to her. "You just are. End of story."

"That's not much of an answer." Audra laughed. Hali just pouted in response. She smiled and reached behind her to grab a basket Hali didn't even know was there. "I brought some food. I'm not sure what you like so I brought a mix of things."

Hali smiled at the gesture. "What do you have?"

Audra rummaged through, pulling a few things out. "I've got some pastries, apples, two ham and cheese sandwiches, and two slices of cake."

"Oh! Human food! I haven't had human food in a long time!" Hali exclaimed, smiling brightly as he took a bite of a sandwich.

Audra took the other sandwich. "Hm. Now that I'm thinking about it, what's siren food like?"

Hali smiled. "Fish! Lots and lots of magically cooked fish! We get to combine fish and sea plants and either cook them with magic or eat them raw. Sometimes you can get birds if they land on the water. Boiled seagull is my favorite!"

"Oh. I didn't know seagulls were edible."

He shrugged. "Maybe it isn't. To humans at least. Sirens and humans look kind of similar but we are different species."

Audra hummed. "Are there any dishes you know of that humans definitely can eat?" she asked.

Hali racked his memory of both meals and also things he knew weren't poisonous. There were a few he could think of. He nodded. "I've got a couple off the top of my head."

She smiled. "Could you make it for me? I'd love to try some of your food."

Hali returned her smile. "I'd love to!" He looked down at the sandwich, a sad smile appearing on his face.

Audra noticed. "Hey, what's wrong?"

"Nothings wrong," Hali replied, lying.

Audra rolled her eyes. "That's a lie and we both know it."

"How did you know?" Hali gasped, throwing his hands up and acting super surprised.

Audra laughed. "I just did. End of story."

That made Hali laugh. "How dare you!" he cried between laughs. "How dare you use my own words against me! Ahh, the betrayal."

The two let their laughter die out a bit before Audra got her serious expression back. "But seriously, are you okay?"

Hali's eyes darkened. "Not really." He mumbled. "Sorry."

"Do you want to talk about it?" she asked.

"Yeah," Hali relented. "I think I should. It's something

I should get off my chest, but it's pretty sad so it's fine if you don't want to listen."

Audra grabbed his hands, turning him to face her. Hali was taken aback by how beautiful she looked in the colorful light of the grotto. Light skin, freckles, and shining light blue eyes. Her light brown hair was pulled back in a loose braid with a few stray hairs falling in her face. "Hali, listen to me. If something is bothering you, you can always come to talk to me. Okay?"

Hali nodded and leaned back on his arms. "Well, I guess I'll start with the easy bit. Don't get me wrong about this, I'm super happy you brought food, but it doesn't really matter. Food isn't filling for sirens. It's something that we can enjoy, yes, but it isn't filling. The only thing that fills us is…"

"Souls," Audra interrupted. "You have to eat souls."

Hali paused, but then nodded and continued. "Yep. It sucks and I don't like doing it, but it's necessary to live. Back… before everything happened, we used to topple enemy ships and eat the souls of criminals. I'm hungry, but I haven't risked eating a soul in a while. And the last time…" He shuddered.

Audra rubbed his shoulder. It was comforting, and Hali leaned into the touch. He felt a stray tear fall down his face. Audra wiped it away with her hand. "You don't have to talk about it if you don't want to."

"No, no. I do. It's just hard to talk about. I'll just explain what happened. The last time I needed a soul, well, it didn't go well. But first I need to talk about Marni. Marni was the type of kid parents would warn their children to stay away from. They went to the surface to gamble, picked fights, and smuggled things for money. But I've always been curious, if not a little reckless. I'd gone straight up to them one day and asked to be friends. Ever since that day, we became pretty much inseparable. We were best friends, almost siblings. Marni and I pulled some dumb stuff, but Marni was always there to protect me if things got out of hand. And I like to think I was good for Marni, too. It was thanks to my pestering that Marni got more responsible and was able to join the royal guard. It wasn't that hard, considering Marni was one of the strongest fighters in the pod. As well as the most bloodthirsty. My mother never exactly liked them but tolerated them for my sake. I hadn't really had many other friends," Hali explained, a small smile coming to his face as he thought of his best friend. The happy memories were still there, but his mood darkened as the bad memories came back.

Audra grabbed his hand and squeezed it. "They sound like a good friend," she said, her voice soft.

Hali smiled. "Yeah, they were."

Audra's smile faltered. "Were?"

"They're gone. And it's my fault."

It was a few weeks after Hali's mother died, and the two of them had been on their own. They were both living in Marni's secret cave hideout. The space was not very big, but not tiny either. There was a large rock blocking the entrance. A large shell bed sat in the center. Swords and other weapons were scattered around, usually resting close to the skulls of their owner. Skulls sat in piles, functioning as shelves and legs of tables. Lanterns were placed precariously on skulls, being lit by Marni's magic.

Hali was starving. He hadn't fed since the purge began. Marni still had energy to spare, as they ate more often than other sirens. Hali had almost no energy, he could barely move. Marni had put him in the shell bed to rest and was now swimming back and forth in a way that would be pacing if they had feet.

"I have an idea," Marni suggested. Hali glanced at them, too tired to do anything. "Don't look at me like that. I'm going to go get you a soul. I'll bring it back in a jar."

Hali smiled weakly. "Like they do for babies?" he asked teasingly.

Marni rolled their eyes. "Well, you are a big baby so it seems fitting." Hali tried to protest but was cut off. "Look, it's the best option we have. It's either that or I let you starve, which I'm not going to do."

"But It's too dangerous!" Hali tried to yell, but it came out as more of a whisper. He tried to move towards Marni, but only managed to fall to the floor. Marni used magic to lift him back up onto the bed. They tied their bright orange hair back and slipped on the admiral's jacket they had taken from one of their victims.

They picked up their trident and smiled. "Wow, do you have that little faith in me? I'm hurt. I'll be fine, Hali. I'll come back and bring you some food so we can get up and out of here."

"Promise?" Hali mumbled. "Promise you won't die?"

Marni's eyes widened. "I promise," they answered before swimming out, closing the door behind them.

Hali didn't know how long it was before Marni came

back. He had drifted into an uneasy sleep, plagued by nightmares he could no longer remember. When he did wake up, he was too tired and could barely focus. He didn't try to move again, knowing full well it was pointless. Marni had left. He could only hope and pray. He didn't even know who he was praying to, he didn't have enough energy to think that far. If any of the gods heard him, they would just hear a bunch of nonsense that vaguely sounded like a call for help.

When Marni did return, Hali didn't notice until there was the rim of a jar being pressed against his lips. He slurped up the liquid, immediately feeling energized again. He looked up at Marni, seeing them smiling down at him. "Marni?" He questioned. He scooted back and took in their entire figure. His eyes widened. There was a massive stab wound on Marni's stomach.

Marni started to tip over, but Hali was quick to catch them. His breathing quickened as he examined the wound. "Hey, Hali. Sorry, it took so long."

"Don't apologize right now, you idiot! You're bleeding!" Hali scolded. He quickly cast a healing spell. It didn't work.

"Royal Guard. He had an enchanted blade," Marni explained. Hali cursed and tried another healing spell.

"Stop, Hali. Don't waste your energy," Marni said.

"You're dying!" Hali screamed.

"I know. And it's fine."

Hali glared at them. "No, it's not! It's not fine! I'm not going to let you die. How can you think this is fine?!??"

Marni sighed and leaned their head back. "Because you'll live." That shut Hali up. "I've had a good run. It's been fun.

But all good things come to an end. It's my time. And if you get to keep living, that's fine with me. Just, keep going, okay? Stay alive. My story might be over but yours is just beginning."

"Marni, please! Hold on!" Hali sobbed.

Marni laughed. "Sorry. It's too late for that, guppy." Hali hugged Marni, sobbing into their chest. "Don't cry, please. You're not a baby," Marni scolded. Hali quickly tried to stop his crying but felt the tears continue anyway. "Hali? Thank you. Thank you for being my friend." They closed their eyes, and Hali saw the lights go out. That only meant one thing. Marni was dead.

Hali stayed in that room for a long time, holding onto Marni's lifeless body. At some point, he got up and used magic to bury their body beneath the rock of the cave. Then, he solemnly cleaned Marni's trident and embedded it into the floor. He laid back on the kelp bed, crying himself to sleep and barely getting up. It was a long time before he left the cave, and by the time he finally got off his tail, the wall was already up and everyone else was gone.

"So, yeah. My best friend died because of me. If I could have been stronger or gone up by myself, maybe they'd still be alive," Hali choked out. He didn't exactly remember when he'd started crying, but at some point he had.

He felt someone wrap their arms around him, and he wrapped his arm around the other person. Vaguely, he realized it was Audra. She whispered comforting words, and let Hali cry.

Prince Cassius of Aurelian had a lot to think about. He was

sitting on the window seat in the guest bedroom he was currently occupying, with a clear sphere of what looked like glass in his hand. It had only been one day in Carnelian, and he already had a wrench in his plan.

And that wrench had a name. Princess Audra of Carnelian. He had expected her to be a lot more entitled. A majority of princesses he had met were rude and arrogant, but surprisingly, she had actually been quite nice. When her father and that arrogant Prince Ajax made Mel cry, she came to check up on him. Later, the three of them had a very pleasant lunch.

Cassius had not come to this kingdom with the intention of marrying its princess. He was already in a committed relationship with Mel anyway. The original intention of his coming was to stage a coup and take over the country. That plan included killing both the king and the princess. Now, he wasn't sure he wanted to kill Audra. She seemed nice and didn't share her father's ideals. It was something he would have to bring up with Ruler Athos.

Speaking of which, the clear ball in his hands started to glow. It filled with the gold mist Cassius knew was Athos's magic before being replaced with their face. "Cassius. Child, I hope your trip has been acceptable."

Cassius smiled. Athos had always been a prominent figure in his life ever since he was a child. They kept things professional in front of others but behind closed doors, Athos was almost like his grandparent. They had never had kids of their own and treated his parents as if they were their own children. "Hello, Athos. It's been interesting, to say the least.

How are you? I trust you made it to the gate safely?"

"Yes. My troops are safe, we had no unordinary encounters on the way here. What we found when we got here was interesting as well," they responded.

Cassius raised an eyebrow. "Really? What did you find?"

Athos sighed. "The situation here is worse than what we were led to believe." Cassius's eyes widened as they continued. "We knew it was a slaughter, but we thought there were still some sirens who had managed to avoid death."

"No... They're all gone?"

Athos shook his head no, and for a brief moment, there was a flicker of hope. "Cassius, there's only one siren left. And he's a kid. Can't be older than 17."

Cassius felt his breath go short. "No..." he muttered. "All those people..."

Athos nodded solemnly. "We can only hope some of them left. I know sirens are territorial but they should have at least sent the children away. The Evergreen Sea Pod wasn't large but it wasn't tiny either. I know some sirens from there ended up in my pod. They were mostly ones who had small children, but even then it was only four or five families."

"What about the siren still here? Is he alright?"

"Right now? He's alright. No injuries. He looks like he hasn't eaten a soul in a while, but he's in no immediate danger. But he did say something very strange."

Cassius raised an eyebrow. "What did he say?"

"He said Princess Audra was his friend," Athos replied.

"Well, that is unexpected," Cassius stuttered out. It took a lot to surprise him, but a siren being friends with the princess of the kingdom that massacred them was enough to throw him for a loop. Even if he had thought the princess was more than what they had first thought, this was a little much.

Athos nodded. "It is. I explained our plan to him, but he got defensive when I said we planned to kill the princess. The child seems to care about her."

Cassius's shock settled. "Well, as shocked as I am, it lines up. Princess Audra was much different than what we had expected."

Athos raised an eyebrow. "Oh? Do tell me more."

"Well, she's nice. Considerate," Cassius explained, then scowled. "Unlike some people. Ajax of Grenoria is very rude and inconsiderate. So is the king. They both intentionally made Mel uncomfortable. Mel fled the room and I followed. She came and apologized for her father's actions. We had lunch with her and she was very nice, if not a little passionate. She'd make a good ruler."

Athos nodded thoughtfully. "This does change things."

"It doesn't need to change too much. We can still go with the original plan. But this time we should involve Audra. We're no longer taking Carnelian over for Audelion, we're dethroning the king so a better ruler can take his place." Cassius explained. Not much needed to be changed. Obviously, some things would switch seeing as the princess was involved, but it was something they could work with.

"I'll inform my troops. For now, If my memory serves

me correctly you have a job to do," Athos reminded him. Their smile lightened. "Have a nice night, child. Stay safe."

And with that, the sphere the ruler appeared in went blank. Cassius sighed, a light smile on his face. He stood up, opened his trunk, and hid the sphere under some clothes. He changed out of his prince clothes and put on a normal outfit. He grabbed a black cloak, swinging it over his shoulders and pulling the hood up before opening the window to sneak out. He had a revolution to gather.

CHAPTER 7

udra was a bit nervous, to say the least. It had been a few days, and she and Hali had decided it was time to introduce her to Cassius and Mel. Audra had spent most of the days hiding with them, and the three had grown closer over that time. She trusted them, and while Hali was apprehensive, she trusted Audra so she was willing to trust them.

Now, Audra was standing in front of Cassius's door. She was smiling, happy to introduce her royal friends to her awesome siren friend. She knocked on the door. It was early in the morning, and she honestly wasn't expecting him to be up. "Who is it?" She heard him yell through the door.

"It's Audra!" she yelled back. She heard grumbling from the other side and then finally he opened the door.

"What do you want milady? It's rather early?" he asked.

"Can I come in? This isn't something we should discuss where anyone could overhear us," she answered. He moved out of the way, politely holding the door open. She was only mildly surprised to see Mel curled up in the bed. She quickly looked over and was at least grateful they were both wearing sleep clothes. "I take it you've met before?" she teased, raising her eyebrow for effect.

Cassius rolled his eyes but smiled fondly and nodded. "We have. Aureolin is significantly closer to Cerulean than it is to Carnelian. I've attended quite a few balls and events in their kingdom and Mel has done the same in mine. I guess you could say we're good friends."

Audra resisted the urge to roll her eyes at Cassius calling Mel a good friend. *Yeah right,* she thought. *I might not know much about friends but I'm relatively certain good friends don't sleep in the same bed.*

"So," Cassius asked, closing the door behind him as they walked further into the room. He kept his voice low, obviously trying to not wake up the sleeping prince. "What brings you here this early in the morning?"

Audra smiled. "There's someone I want you to meet. Both of you. We'll tell my father we're going on a ride, and not to expect us for lunch. I'll take you two out to meet them."

The corners of Cassius's mouth quirked up in what she had figured out was a smirk. "I'd love to meet them, and I'm sure Mel would feel the same way."

Audra's smile grew. "Thank you."

He turned away, pretending to be in deep thought. "Though, I am perplexed. I wasn't aware you had any other friends."

She glared playful before they both chuckled. "Can it, rich boy. I do have other friends. And with the word 'other,' you're implying that we're friends."

Now it was Cassius's turn to glare. "I said no such thing."

Audra shrugged. "You implied it."

They heard someone groan, a groggy noise as if they were just getting out of bed. Both royals turned their heads to see Mel sitting up. His orange hair was a mess, and he didn't seem to be fully awake yet. "Cass? What's going on?" he slurred.

Cassius smiled. "Nothing to worry about, my dear. Audra just decided to stop by."

Mel grinned and rubbed the sleep from his eyes. "Hey Audra! What are you doing here? And this early, too?" he asked as he swung off the bed, making his way to the vanity to grab a brush.

"I wanted you two to meet a friend of mine. She's a little ways away, so we're going on a ride and bringing a picnic," Audra explained.

"Yay! A new friend. I was wondering if you had any others," Mel exclaimed.

"Hey! I have friends!" Audra yelled, a little annoyed. "Why does everybody think I don't have friends!"

"Since we've been here you've spent quite a lot of time with us. If you had other friends you would hang out with them," Cassius answered, keeping his face serious.

Audra huffed. "It was rhetorical."

"Oh. My apologies," he joked.

The three giggled. "Well, I'll leave you two love birds to get changed," she said, making her way to the door. She would cherish the massive blush Mel got and Cassius's vaguely surprised expression forever. "What? It's not like it was hard to put together. You two make a nice couple. I'm happy for you."

"You're not mad? We're supposed to court you," Mel asked quietly.

Audra grumbled. "I'm not mad at you. I don't want to be courted in the first place. That was my father's idea." She stopped grumbling. "Speaking of which, please don't tell my father we're meeting someone. If he asks it's just going to be the three of us."

Cassius looked suspicious, but nodded. Mel looked a bit confused, but also nodded. "Alright. Should we be worried we're going somewhere illegal?"

Audra shrugged. "Kind of? It's nothing dangerous, I promise, But there's a reason I don't want my father to know who I'm meeting with."

Mel smiled. "Okay. Just don't kill us please."

She smiled back and walked out the door. She had a bit of time before breakfast, so she decided to go start making them a picnic basket. She was wearing her riding clothes already. She wanted to head out as quickly as possible. Unfortunately, fate had other plans. Rather, Prince Ajax had other plans.

"Princess Audra!" She heard him before she saw him. She whipped around. He was standing in the hall, obviously having just left his room. Though why he needed to wear armor before breakfast was beyond her. He seemed to always be wearing it. She didn't even bother replying to him, simply rolling her eyes and kept walking. Ajax, however, didn't like that. "Princess!" he called, and ran to catch up with her. The blonde fell into step beside her.

"What do you want, Ajax?" she grumbled. He had been nothing but forceful and annoying since he had arrived. She was constantly dodging him and rejecting his advances. Mel and Cassius had helped with that, but the dude just couldn't seem to see she wasn't interested. At all.

Ajax put on that slimy smile he always had when trying to get her attention. "Well, I want you to come watch me spar with the knight. When we get married I'll be leading the troops, so of course you'll have to stand beside me as I command them, like a good wife."

Audra froze. *He did not just say that,* she thought. She stopped walking and turned to face him. "Ajax. I'm not going to marry you. Nothing you do will convince me."

The prince sneered. "You'd rather have that crybaby?" he said, talking about Mel. "Or that weakling?" Now he mentioned Cassius. He rolled his eyes. "I know girls are stupid but I didn't think you were that dumb." His tone was patronizing and it made Audra's blood boil. "Listen, I know it's hard but I'm obviously the better choice."

"And why would that be?" she asked, knowing full well she wouldn't like the answer.

He smirked and puffed up his chest proudly. "Because I'm stronger than both of them. And I'm better at night, if you know what I mean."

You know what, that's it. I was trying to be nice but that's inappropriate and out of line. "Ajax," she said, voice cold. She grabbed both his shoulders. "I'm going to make one thing very clear to you." She brought her knee up with as much force as possible into his groin. His face immediately contorted in pain, and Audra giggled because it looked like he just drank straight lemon juice. "I. Do. Not. Like. You! I do not want to talk to you! Your advances are unwanted. Maybe i would have liked you if you weren't such a rude, inconsiderate piece of horse feces. But you are, and no one with an ounce of respect would want to share a bed, much less marry the pile of horse poop shaped like a human that is you and your slimy personality. Have. A. Good. Day."

She let him drop to the floor, where he stayed, clutching his groin. She smiled as she walked away. *What a baby.* And, without a second thought, she kept walking to her destination.

Breakfast was an awkward affair to say the least. Ajax wasn't glaring at her, he was glaring at both Mel and Cassius. When they told her father they were going on a ride, he had almost had an outburst, but a glare from Audra shut him down real fast. All in all, she was glad it was over.

"I will take a guess and say something happened between you and Prince Ajax," Cassius asked. They had left a little while ago, and were now riding to the usual meeting place. She had asked Hali if it was okay to bring them there, and they said it was fine. Audra rode on Victory, her horse, while Cassius rode on a sleek white stallion named Blizzard and Mel had picked a brown mare named Flora. He said he liked the flower name. They weren't dressed fancily. Cassius still looked wealthy, in his fine white linen tunic and black pants with leather boots. But Mel was surprisingly wearing something relatively normal. He had on a slightly stained, loose brown tunic and patched brown pants. She shouldn't have been surprised. Mel wasn't born a royal, and chances were he had been extremely poor before becoming prince.

Audra smirked. "I may or may not have kneed him in the balls." Mel laughed and Cassius snorted. Audra held her hands out in defense. "I'm not saying I did, but if I did it was super satisfying."

"Well, I'm glad you did. I'm not saying you didn't, but if you hadn't I might have," Cassius remarked, making all three laugh again.

"Cass!" Mel cried, trying to look mad but also laughing.

The forest was different in the daylight. Brighter. It had a more upbeat vibe than it did in the nighttime. The sun was out today, unblocked by clouds and only slightly risen in the sky. Dew clung to the plants, shining like jewels. The ground was damp. Here and there, squirrels climbed up trees and they even saw a deer. It smelled like fresh rain and pine. Early morning birds called.

Audra smiled, tilting her head back and taking in the beauty of her kingdom. She loved it. All of it, even if some of the people annoyed her. It was all part of Carnelian's charm. A question popped into her head. "Hey, guys, what are your kingdoms like? I've never been, so I don't know."

Mel beamed. "Cerulean's beautiful! Oh, gods, I could go on for hours about how much I love it. There's only one big city, the capital. The city is all in these giant walls with the castle in the middle. The rest of the kingdom is small, spread-out villages. It's all rolling hills and farmland. Actually, I was very surprised to see how many trees you have here. We have trees, but not this many in one place. Mostly it's farmland and meadows," he explained animatedly. Audra had noticed he moved his hand around a lot when talking.

"It sounds amazing. I'd love to see it sometime," Audra said. She looked over at Cassius, who was watching Mel with a smile on his face. She chuckled. "Hey, Cass!" she called, starling him out of his trance. "What's Andelian like?"

Cassius got this small smile on his face. "Well," he started, "it's home. We've got a mountain range that runs through the middle of our kingdom. The side closest to the water is a lot like here, actually, but less cold. The other half is more of a desert because we are in a rainshadow. It's a lot more rocky and sandy over there. Much fewer trees. Mostly, there are bushes and small bits of grass. It's not as beautiful as this is by any means, but I love it."

Before she could say anything, she spotted the rock ledge. "We're here," she said, dismounting her horse. Cassius and Mel soon followed. Audra led the two of them to the ridge.

"I don't see anyone here. Are you sure this is the place?" Cassius asked.

Audra just smiled. *"Hey, Hali! We're here!"* she yelled. She giggled when Cassius and Mel gasped. A small waterfall trickled over the ledge, forming a floating platform that partly solidified. "Well," she smirked, "after you."

Cassius was the first person to break out of his stupor. He calmly stepped onto the platform, obviously having been used to this. Mel looked a bit hesitant but stepped on when he saw that Cassius was safe. Audra hopped on after, and the platform started to levitate. It was shaky, and if Audra hadn't done this before she would have been scared they would fall off. Mel, however, hadn't done this before. He screamed and clung to Cassius, who for his part was doing quite well at masking his own fear.

Soon enough, they made it to the grotto. It too was different in the day. The plants didn't glow, yet it still had a magical energy. The water made an almost perfect mirror of the sky. The rock ledges casted shadows here and there. But, most stunning of all, was Hali. She was wearing a new shirt, a loose purple tank top, as well as a purple sash around where her waist would be. Her blonde hair was pulled back into a ponytail with more shiny purple fabric. She smiled when they entered.

"Hello, Audra's friends!" she called. Both boys froze. Their eyes widened. Hali pouted, crossing her arms over her chest. "Audra! You didn't tell them about me? I thought we were friends!" she joked.

Mel laughed. "Well, I can't say I'm not surprised." He walked forward, offering his hand to shake. "I'm Mel. What's your name?"

Hali shook his hand firmly. "I'm Hali. I'm glad to meet you." She smiled.

Cassius didn't come forward, but his posture did lose most of its stiffness. "My name is Cassius. This is most certainly not what I was expecting." He turned to Audra. "A little warning next time would be nice."

Audra merely laughed. She took off her boots and rolled up her pant legs. She sat on the edge of the water, putting her feet in and sitting on the edge. Hali swam around her, hoisting herself onto the ledge so they could sit next to each other. She smirked. "So, do you believe in love at first sight or do I have to swim by again?"

"Oh c'mon." Audra giggled as she punched Hali lightly on the arm. "These are just getting worse every time!"

"Oh, you know you like my pickup lines! If you didn't, you wouldn't be blushing!" Hali laughed.

Mel, who had sat on the rocks next to Audra, laughed. "She's right you know. You are blushing." He paused and turned to Hali. "You go by her, right?"

Hali nodded. "Right now, yes. I'll tell you guys if that changes. Thanks."

"No problem."

"So," Cassius started. "Audra, Hali, not that I'm unhappy to meet you, but I'm wondering why?"

Hali shrugged. "I was lonely. There really isn't much of a reason other than that."

Mel nodded thoughtfully. "Understandable. I do have a few questions, though."

"Ask away!" She smiled.

"So, how did you two meet?" he asked.

Audra and Hali made eye contact and then burst out laughing. It was stressful at first, but looking back on the events that led to them being friends it was quite funny. "It's a bit of a story," Audra started. "I ran into her in the market, accidentally found this place later that day, and then we started talking."

Cassius raised an eyebrow. "And how long ago was this?" he asked, trying to make sense of what was going on.

"Like, four days ago," Hali said offhandedly, waving it off. "So! What's your guys' deal?"

Cassius didn't press it but looked skeptical. Audra couldn't really blame him. It was a really strange situation, and she did kind of spring this on him. Mel too. They were actually taking all this quite well. They made small talk and ate the food Audra had brought. Everything started out a bit awkward, but the awkwardness faded soon and the four were able to talk as if they were old friends. A calm atmosphere fell over the group, and they talked for a long while before it was broken.

"Hey, Cass?" Mel asked. They'd come to a quiet spot in the conversation, and Mel looked like he just remembered something important.

"Hm?" Cassius answered.

"When we went down to the town yesterday, did you notice how we didn't see many magical beings? I think in the entire time we were down there I only saw one hive," he exclaimed.

Cassius paused, trying to remember. "Actually, now that you mention it, I didn't see any non-humans either. It's strange."

Audra was confused. "What do you mean? Non-humans?"

"Like sirens?" Hali added.

"Wait, You don't know about non-humans?"

Mel exclaimed.

Both girls shook their heads. "I feel like I've heard of magical beings other than sirens before, but I can't remember where," Hali explained.

"Yeah, I've read about them, but I just thought they were a mainland thing. Or stayed in one place like sirens," Audra agreed.

Cassius shook his head. "No. They used to live in certain places—depending on species—but now mostly they live in cities."

"And it's not just a mainland thing!" Mel added. "There's a lot of hives and fairies in Cerulean."

"Fairies? Hives?" Hali asked, incredulously

Mel looked dumbstruck. "There really aren't other species in Carnelian."

"Huh. That is definitely strange." Cassius sighed. "Especially because this island has a mountain. At the very least there should be avians."

"Okay. Now you've rattled my brain. A quick explanation of what those species are would be good," Audra aired. She turned and laid her head on Hali's lap, who immediately started running her fingers though Audra's hair. Her brain hurt.

"Fairies are small creatures that live in flower fields. They look humanoid but with different colored skin and hair as well as bug-like wings. They tend to live in either forests or flower fields," Mel explained. "Hives are living bug hives. They look like humans, but have holes in their bodies where the bugs can enter from. Sometimes they have different features depending on what bug they host. They also tend to stay in fields, and even help out with pollination of the crops."

Cassius continued for him. "avians are bird-human hybrids. The have feathers on their arms that allow them to fly as well as talons for feet. They have feathers on their face similar to Hali's scales. They live on mountains and keep them safe."

"Which is why it's weird that there aren't any avians on Carnelian. There should be some to protect the mountain. Unless they stay up there?" Mel finished.

Audra shook her head, scowling. "No, there aren't. We have military posts all around the mountain, almost to the summit. We would have noticed." She huffed. "I don't like the implications of this."

"What implications?" asked Mel.

Hali looked grim. "That they were wiped out. Like the rest of the sirens."

No one spoke after that. There wasn't much to say. It was a theory, hopefully, but none of them could deny its weight. If it was true... Audra didn't know what that would do. She really, really hoped it wasn't. The air was tense, all of them stewing in their thoughts. No one seemed to be willing to break the silence.

Luckily, Hali's stomach did that for them. It rumbled, loudly. The sound rang out through the silence. All eyes turned to Hali, and she quickly covered her stomach with her hands and smiled sheepishly. "Sorry..." she mumbled.

Audra sat up. "Don't apologize."

"You haven't eaten in a while," Cassius observed. It

was a statement, not a question. Hali just nodded, still embarrassed. "Well, we'll have to fix that."

Hali tilted her head to the side, looking at him confused. "Wait, what?"

Cassius looked very confident in his words. "You haven't eaten in a while. If you don't eat something soon you'll lose strength. Based on that rumble and the bags under your eyes you've already started losing strength. We can't have that. We'll get you a soul."

Mel's eyes widened. He shook his head wildly. "Whoa whoa whoa! Where'd this 'we' come from? I never agreed to be a part of this."

Cassius raised an eyebrow. "Really? Usually, you jump right on board when it comes to helping people."

"Not when helping involves killing someone!"

"You've done it before," Cassius soothed, placing a soothing hand on Mel's shoulder. They stared into each other's eyes, seemingly having a silent conversation. Hali and Audra just waited awkwardly for them to finish.

Eventually, Mel sighed and put his head in his hands. "I know. But I had to then. We were at war. I don't want to kill anyone ever again."

Hali smiled and put a hand on his shoulder. "I understand. If it helps, you won't be the one to kill them. I'll do that part."

"You don't have to help if you don't want to," Audra assured him. "All we ask is that you stay quiet."

Mel thought for a moment, wringing his hands on his pants. "Alright," he decided. "I'll help."

Cassius gave him a reassuring smile, before turning to face the rest of the group. "We need to decide on who we let Hali eat. Any ideas, Audra?"

Audra smirked. "I have one. Ajax."

"You want to kill a prince from another kingdom," Cassius stated, giving Audra a disappointed stare. "That's practically asking for war."

Audra shrugged. "Not unless we make it look like an accident. Leave it to me. I've got an idea."

Cassius sighed, shaking his head. "Alright fine. I sincerely hope you know what you are doing. Anyone opposed?" No one said anything. "Well then, we have a prince to kill."

Chapter 8

Prince Ajax of Grenoria was a prideful man, and what he wanted he would get. Eventually. Sometimes it was a new robe, other times it was to win a battle or place high in a tournament. He always got what he wanted. And right now, he wanted to marry Princess Audra. And he would. He was sure off it.

Audra had so far been very rude to him, but he knew that didn't say anything about his chances with her. Girls were so temperamental. They always played hard to get. The real challenge was to get her father to like you, and then he would convince her to like you. He already felt pretty accomplished in this step, as he had been invited to have lunch with the king. Audra would not be joining them, as she had decided to have lunch with the traitor and that gutter rat pretending to be a prince. He knew girls were foolish when it came to men, but even she should know better than to fall for those disgusting fools. No matter. When he was her husband he would make sure they never bothered her again.

He pushed open the door to a smaller dining room

than the one they ate breakfast in, not bothering to knock. The king was waiting for him, and he looked up when he entered the room. "Ah, Prince Ajax. Have a seat."

Ajax sat down in the chair across from him and studied the king. He was old, as he could tell by the lines on his face and the gray in his hair. He had been a strong fighter once, but those days are long gone. He looked weak. Yet, still, he had an air of strength and superiority around him. Ajax could respect that. The king was a strong leader, the kind Ajax wished he could be.

"So, how has your stay been so far?" the king asked.

"Good," he answered. "Carnelian is beautiful, sir."

"Thank you. My family has worked hard to keep it that way." He took a sip from his goblet. Ajax couldn't see what it was, but he could guess and say it was wine. That's what made the most sense for it to be, anyway. "Say, Ajax. Would you say Carnelian is clean?"

Ajax thought for a second. There were still peasants, of course. And the houses were still dull and muddy. But Carnelian looked cleaner. More presentable. "Yes. It is."

"Good good," the king muttered, and Ajax shifted a bit in his seat. "You know," the king started, "my wife died years ago."

"My condolences on your loss. It must have been hard, to lose a wife."

"It was. My wife was beautiful. She was *mine*. No one should ever have been able to take her away from me. Much less those ... *vermon*." He spit out the word like it hurt him to say.

"How did she die, if I may ask?"

The king sighed. "She was murdered by sirens."

Ajax gasped. "Really? I was not aware of that."

"Not many people are, and that is by design. I ask that you keep this between us."

"I will, I promise you," he told him.

The king nodded. "Good." He sighed and leaned back in his chair. "My wife had been taken by sirens long before that, though. I owned everything of hers. Yet her heart was stolen from me by their leader. I let her play her little game with him. I let the two have their fun. Then, they had a falling out and she begged to go home to visit her family. And on her way," he took a breath, something that sounded almost like a held-back sob, "her ship was attacked. By sirens. They killed her, after all the love she had shown them."

The king took a sip of his wine, and Ajax nodded. "They are cruel, cruel creatures."

"I'm glad you understand, Ajax, what I'm trying to do here. What I'm trying to keep my people safe from. What my family has tried to keep safe for generations."

"I do," Ajax agreed. "I really do, your highness."

"My question for you, Ajax," the king said, and Ajax knew that this question would be what made Audra his. What would determine the king's opinion of him for all of time to come. "Are you prepared to continue our family's hard fight?"

"I am, your highness," he answered with as much certainty as he could muster. "I am."

The king smiled, and Ajax knew he had won.

With a plan set in place, Audra waited until after breakfast to set it into motion. What could she say? She wanted to eat some pastries before aiding in a murder. After breakfast was over, she approached Ajax in the hall, putting on the meekest face she could make. "Ajax?" she called.

He spun around, face filling with slight fear, which Audra would admit she did enjoy before he straightened up. "Audra. I didn't see you there," he said, a bit awkwardly but Audra had to admit he was doing a good job of keeping his composure.

She sighed. "I'm actually here to apologize." That shocked him. "What I did was out of line. I'm sorry," she said, making her voice as apologetic as possible. He ate it up, believing every word. Audra smirked. She had always considered herself a good liar. "I was angry at someone else and took my anger out on you. Is there any way I could make it up to you?"

Ajax looked genuinely surprised, but the shock left his face quickly, replaced by one of the gross smirks she'd come to hate. "Well, spending the day with you would be rather enjoyable."

She smiled. "Well, the sun is shining today. A rarity here. How about a boat ride?"

Ajax laughed. "You can't be serious! Not with a siren on the loose. You of all people should know how dangerous they are."

Now it was Audra's turn to laugh. "Between you and me, that's just a rumor. We've been trying to calm the public, especially the servants down, but hysteria is a hard feeling to quell. Plus," she added. "There's nothing to be scared of, I have a big strong man like you to protect me."

That got him. She had hit the mark, feeding directly to his ego. His confidence tripled, and immediately he started leading the way to the royal docks. He went on a tangent about how strong he was. Audra almost rolled her eyes. Most of the stuff he was spewing was either stories from the war between Grenoria and Cerulean or very overexaggerated.

"You!" he barked at one of the servants near the watercraft shed. The servant jumped at his commanding voice. "Fetch us a boat." He demanded. The wide-eyed servant looked confused, obviously not knowing who this was.

Henry, Audra remembered. *That's his name. He's the shipwright's son.* Henry looked at the princess with a questioning glance. As per their plan, the shipwrights had already been asked to prepare a boat for her. A bit of bribery and no one would know the boat was prepared prior to being asked for. His questioning glance was him asking if he should get the boat they prepared. She nodded at him, and he gave a barely concealed sigh before going to retrieve the boat.

"See, that is how you get something you want," Ajax boasted, as if he'd done something to be proud of. "Servants won't listen if you don't give them something to fear. Occasionally you need to put one in their place, just to make an example to the others."

Audra felt a new anger burn in her chest. This guy was talking about servants as if they weren't even human! She felt sick at the thought of hurting one of them. Many of the castle servants had been there when she was down. Ayla, the laundrymaid, would let her hide from her lessons in the laundry room when she was little. Evelyn, the cook, had made her smiley faces out of sauce on days when she was feeling bad. Even her old maid Hanna, the one before Lila, had held her when she needed to cry.

And because they treated her with kindness, she treated them with kindness as well. Listening to Elmer, the gardener, brag about his grandkids. Asking Daniel what was wrong when she saw him wiping away tears while dusting the curtains. And later giving him the day off along with a pouch of gold coins to go take care of his sick kid. Congratulating and giving Franny and Alex a large sack of gold after their wedding. She tried to be kind and helpful. Even if she was strong, she didn't want others to fear her.

She wanted to say something against Ajax, but decided it was better to hold her tongue. He would get what was coming to him. She just had to be patient. Henry came back along with a few other servants, all rowing the small sailboat into the tiny dock just off the shore. It was only used for small watercraft. The servants got out, and Ajax jumped in. He held out his hand and daintily helped her into the boat. She could have just jumped in but was keeping up the delicate little flower act.

She sat down on the small bench and watched as Ajax undid the ropes and pushed the boat away from the dock. "Is there anything I can do to help?" she asked.

Ajax laughed. "You really are a silly girl! Boating is a

men's sport. Women would be too weak for life on the sea. You must keep track of many things, like changing water speeds and wind currents. A woman wouldn't even know where to begin with those things! Don't worry. You just sit back and relax."

Audra had to stifle a laugh. *Yeah right. If you're going to mansplain, at least get your facts right. I don't even think wind currents are a thing.* Really, he should know better. She was the princess of an island nation. At some point, it had been required that she learn how to use a boat. It was a vital skill, and almost everyone in Carnelian knew how.

"Now this," Ajax started, "this puny vessel is nothing compared to the boat we took to get here. We have far larger ships in my country. I have my own ship. It's called the Destroyer. It's huge. I bet you've never seen something so big in your life."

Audra sighed. She had, of course. Carnelian was home to many war vessels. She had been on quite a few. "Oh. It sounds lovely," she said in a bored voice before cursing herself. She had forgotten the act. She prayed to all the gods he didn't notice.

Someone must have heard her, as he started to laugh. "Oh, silly me. You don't know anything about ships. No need to worry. I'll explain everything you need to know." He then started explaining everything about the ship in the most condescending way possible. Audra was starting to get more and more exasperated as he continued. She was extremely grateful when she saw the flip of Hali's tale in the water.

Suddenly, Ajax turned to her. They had gotten far

enough away from the palace that no one could see them. "Well, Princess, it's just the two of us now. And, seeing as you need to repay me for what you did…" He started walking closer to her. Audra just now realized he had put the anchor down and they were stopped. He put his hands on either side of the wall behind her, effectively cornering her. "I don't think anyone will care if I…" He started to lean down to kiss her, and she kicked him in the balls. Again. He groaned, backing up while holding his crotch in pain.

"Absolutely not!" Audra yelled, fury clear in her voice. She raised her foot up and pushed him down, so he was leaning against the front of the boat, almost over the edge with her foot in his face holding him down. "I hated you when I thought you were a rude, arrogant jerk! But then you go trying to kiss me without my consent!? That's crossing a line, buddy. Do you think it's okay to just go kissing girls without their permission because you're a prince? Because guess what! It's not. I hope you burn in the underworld." And with that, she pushed him off the bow of the ship.

He started struggling in the water. But Audra saw Hali poke her head out a little way away and start singing. He immediately stopped struggling, his eyes glossing over. Audra couldn't recognize the words, but she could hear the anger and fury in it. This wasn't a nice song. Hali was mad. And even though the spell wasn't aimed at her she was still slightly terrified.

Hali swam menacingly closer. She grabbed him roughly by the wrist, nothing at all like how she had grabbed Audra when they had first met; and dragged him under and away from the boat. The water stirred angrily around the siren and her prey. Through the choppy water, Audra could see Hali bring her face closer to Ajax. Then, what looked like stings of glowing blue started coming out of his face. Hali opened her mouth and they flowed into her. Audra realized this is what a feeding looks like.

It all happened so fast. One minute everything was going according to plan and the next there was a flash of silver and the song was replaced with a pained scream. "*Hali!*" Audra screamed into the deep water. She tried to see what had happened, but the choppy waves crowded her view. Hali was nowhere in sight, but neither was Ajax. She was about to jump in when a feminine hand shot out of the water, grabbing onto the ship rail.

Audra quickly rushed to pull her up onto the ship. She fell backward, holding a still bleeding Hali in her arms. There was a small gash on her side. "Hey, beautiful," Hali said, wincing in pain afterward.

"Oh, gods. Don't worry, it doesn't look fatal," Audra said, not exactly sure who she was trying to reassure at that point. She quickly grabbed the small med kit on the boat and started to treat the wound. "Also, you've been stabbed. Now is not the time for flirting."

Hali giggled. "It's always time for flirting when it's with you."

Audra blushed a bit, looking away from the other girl's face and down at the wound she was holding pressure to. Suddenly, Hali started shuffling over to the edge of the ship. "Hey! What on earth do you think you're doing?" she yelled.

"I'm healing the wound. I need salt water," Hali answered. Audra sighed and helped her over to the edge. Hali waved her hands around and some water floated upward, seeping into the wound and stopping the bleeding. "That's the best I can do. I'll get some waterproof bandages later. For now," she leaned on Audra, who instinctively wrapped her arms around the smaller girl, "can I stay with you for a while?"

Audra smiled fondly. "Yeah. But only for a little while. I don't know how long it will be until somebody comes by in their boat. Plus, I don't want you aggravating that wound."

"I'll try not to," Hali answered, her voice soft. She stared up into Audra's eyes. Audra stared back.

"What happened?" she asked.

"I lost my hold on the spell," Hali answered. "It was just for a second, but in that time, he pulled out a dagger and stabbed me with the last of his strength. I finished up quickly and he died. I was being reckless. I saw what he tried to do and got possessive, I guess. I was angry."

Audra nodded. "It was pretty terrifying. But in a good way, you know? I'm proud. You looked intimidating. And hot."

Hali blushed and smiled, a bit sadly Audra noticed. "I need to talk to you. Not here, but tonight. Can you meet me at the grotto?"

"Of course. I was planning to come by anyway. We might as well have a bit of a celebration," she responded.

Hali smiled brightly. "Yeah. That sounds fun. Just us, right?"

Audra nodded. "Yeah. Just us." She stood up. "I should head back," she said, a bit awkwardly.

Hali chuckled awkwardly. "Yeah, I'll see you tonight." And with that, she dived into the water and disappeared into its depths. Audra smiled and then started bringing the boat back to shore.

Audra had really gone all out to make this convincing. Crocodile tears ran down her cheeks, and her face held a horrified and haunted expression. When she pulled into the tiny dock again, she was met with servants running at her. "Princess Audra! Are you alright?" Henry asked. He quickly looked over the ship when his eyes widened. Audra panicked for a second, but a slight nod from him told her he wouldn't tell anyone.

"Inform the king," she said, her voice laced with fake sadness. "That Prince Ajax was killed by the siren."
Shocked gasps echoed from around her. One of them ran to go tell the king. Henry offered her an arm, and she leaned against it. "I saw the blood," he whispered. "Purple blood." Audra froze. "Don't worry. I won't tell anyone. No one else will, either. If anyone else asks, the boat was damaged in the attack. Someone is already taking it away to be destroyed," he finished.

Audra calmed down. "Why? You'd willingly lie to your king?" she asked.

Audra could swear she saw the ghost of a smile across his lips. "When you need help, tell Lila that you need Warren's luck. She'll know what to do. It's time you know the truth."

Audra nodded. "Thank you."

Interrupting the moment, the king came running towards the shore, followed closely behind by Cassius and

Mel. "Audra!" he yelled. "What happened?"

Audra turned up the waterworks. "Ajax invited me out on the water. I went with him because he said he would protect me. But then the siren attacked! I was too scared to see but when I opened my eyes the ship was broken, and he was nowhere to be found."

"Oh, gods..." Mel muttered. Cassius looked at her with a raised eyebrow, and she winked. He smiled a bit before his cold façade replaced any hint of amusement.

Her father remained cold as ever, quickly turning to the servants and a few assembled guards. "Send word to the royal family of Grenoria. Inform them that a terrible accident has occurred. Send search parties out to try and find the body." He then turned to the princes. "Help my daughter to her room. I need to deal with important matters." He then left. All the servants returned to what they were doing before. Cassius extended an arm and Audra took it. She and the two princes then walked off in the direction of her room.

When they reached an empty hallway, Audra unhooked her arm and straightened up. She let the act drop and a big smile spread across her face. "Well, that was fun."

Cassius sighed and shook his head, an amused smile on his face. "I take it Hali got fed?"

Audra skipped down the hall a bit. "Yes. We're going to go on a date to celebrate later!"

"A date? Really?" Mel smiled, running up next to her. *He looks uneasy,* she thought. She could understand. He was uneasy about the whole 'killing someone' thing. She nodded at him. "That's good. So you two are dating?"

Audra froze and blushed. "No? Not officially. I mean, I would like to be, but it just won't work right now. There's too much going on. It's too dangerous."

Mel smiled sadly. "I understand. Cassius and I couldn't start dating until after the war was over."

"Yes." Cassius sighed. "I'm glad we did, though. Dating you was the best decision I've ever made."

"It is? Really?" Mel teased.

"Yes," Cassius answered. "Always." And then he leaned in for a kiss.

"Speaking of the fact that you two are in love," Audra interrupted awkwardly. "Can I tell Hali? I won't tell anyone else," she promised.

Cassius nodded. "That would be acceptable." Audra just nodded, and they continued on their way.

CHAPTER 9

It was later that night when Hali lifted Audra up and into the grotto. He was sitting in his usual spot, running his hands over his scales in stress. It was mostly calming, but occasionally he'd space out a bit and get dragged kicking and screaming back to reality when he'd accidentally flip one of his scales the wrong way and end up crying out because of pain. Scales were strong but when they moved or pulled, they caused a lot of pain. Removing scales was considered the worst form of torture, only reserved for the worst sort of criminals.

Hali was pulled from his thoughts by Audra, who took a seat next to him. He chuckled. "I love your outfit. It's so*fish*ticated."

Audra rolled her eyes, a soft smile on her lips. "That has to be one of the worst ones you've come up with so far."

He shrugged. "I will admit, that's not my best work."

Audra just laughed, her face a bit red. "So, I brought some cake and a flask of apple cider."

Hali smiled and took a cup Audra had poured. "Thanks."

Audra tilted her head and looked confused. "Are you okay?" she asked. She put both hands on Hali's shoulders, looking him up and down. "Does your wound hurt? Is something else wrong?"

"What are you talking about?" Hali stuttered, attempting to lie. He cursed himself. He could usually lie reasonably well, but not to Audra. He couldn't lie to Audra.

"That just confirms it. Somethings wrong," Audra announced. Her eyes softened. "I won't force you to tell me, but is there anything I can do to make it better?"

Hali smiled sadly. This wasn't a conversation he wanted to have, much less one he thought he would ever be having. *There's no point in beating around the kelp.* He took a deep breath. "It's actually why I wanted to talk to you. You remember when I was in the town, right?"

Audra laughed, and Hali couldn't help but think that it was the most beautiful sound in the world. "How could I forget? You made a very memorable introduction."

He chuckled. "I told you I was looking for a way out. What I didn't tell you was that I had found one."

Audra froze. Hali looked down at her hands, ashamed. He could see sadness pour into Audra's eyes, and he hated that he had caused it.

"How long?" Audra asked after a moment of silence.

"What?"

"How long until you have to leave?" she clarified. Her voice was cold and detached, making Hali shrink.

"Two days," he answered.

Audra stood up and started pacing, pinching the

bridge of her nose. "And you didn't think to tell me?!" She stomped. Hali flinched, and Audra softened. she sat back down and sighed, leaning back so she was laying on the hard ground.

"I'm sorry. I wanted to tell you! But I was scared," he stuttered out, being interrupted by barely concealed sobs.

"What were you so scared of? Why would telling me to be all that bad!" she cried out.

"Yes!" Hali threw his arm up.

"Why!"

"I was scared you would leave! *Okay!?*" Hali screamed, all his frustration bubbling up to the surface. If either of them were paying attention they would have noticed the water in the lagoon had started to churn. But they didn't, too caught up in their emotions. "I was worried that if you knew I couldn't stay you'd not want to be around me. You wouldn't want to get to know me because I'd be gone and you'd miss me. Cut your losses early, I guess. It was selfish of me not to tell you. It'd only hurt you in the end. But I want to be selfish. I wanted to pretend this, whatever we have, wouldn't end. I wanted to pretend all the bad things didn't exist and it was just you and I. Hold on to this place, my home, and everything I used to love about it—still do love about it—for a little while longer, before I have to leave it all behind."

Audra looked shocked but then sighed, laying back down on the rocks. Hali sighed too, looking away and sliding back into the water. Not completely but enough that just his head was the only thing out of the water. He let the water's energy flow through him.

"You'd be safer if you left, right?" Audra whispered. She rolled her head so both their faces were only inches apart.

Hali nodded, not trusting his voice at the moment. Tears pooled at the edges of his eyes, hot and purple.

"Then you should leave."

"Really?"

Audra nodded, as well as she could while laying on the ground at least. "I want you to be safe. And If that means I can't keep you here with me, then so be it. I'll miss you, but your safety is more important."

Hali smiled softly. "I'll miss you. Really, I will. You've made me so happy these past few days. Happier than I've been in a long time."

In this quiet moment, the calm after the storm, the most unexpected thing happened. Audra rolled over so she was laying on her stomach, and kissed Hali. It was soft, not forceful, as if she was asking for permission. And Hali let her. He smiled into the kiss. They pulled apart, and Audra smiled sheepishly. "I just... wanted to do that. Once, at least. I'm sorry. I should have asked you first. It was wrong of me to do that out of nowhere."

Hali beamed at her, blushing like crazy. "Well... that was something," he said awkwardly. "I liked it, though."

Audra nodded. She was also blushing. "Me too." She took a deep breath. "Look, I'm going, to be honest, I really fancy you. I love your smile, I love your laugh, I love hearing your voice. Hey! I even love your cheesy pickup lines. You're just so uniquely you, it's beautiful! You make me feel amazing, and I don't know what to do with these feelings. But I wanted to tell you before you left. In case I never get the chance to tell you."

"I feel the same way," Hali said, smiling sheepishly. "You make me feel safe. I like being around you because you're so cool. I trust you. You laugh at my jokes and let me talk about my feelings without judgment. Marni was the only other person who would do that. I don't understand it, and in all honesty, it frightens me, but I trust you easily. I'd find it hard not to trust you."

Audra beamed and leaned in to lightly kiss him again. "I'm glad you do." Out of nowhere, Hali laughed. "What are you laughing at? We just shared our hearts with each other and you're laughing."

"Exactly!" he shouted in between giggles. "Wow! This conversation has been one hell of a whirlpool!"

"What does that mean?" Audra asked.

"Well, we started with eating food and being happy, then we were fighting, then we *kissed* and were talking about how we love each other and all that. We change topics *rapidly*." He laughed.

Audra laughed along with him. "You're right. What a weird conversation." She sat up, sitting crisscrossed on the rocks. She reached back to the food she had brought, and pulled out a cake. Hali took it and took a bite, lightning up at the sweet flavor. "I do want you to stay. I'll miss talking to you," she stated.

Hali paused. "Actually, I have an idea." He set his cake down on the rock. "Wait here. I might be a minute," he told her, and then dove down into the water. He swam out of the grotto, passing the rock carvings and emerging in a field of kelp. He slowed down when we reached the plants, careful not to get caught in the leaves. He passed fish and other creatures, who carefully skirted out of his way as he passed. It wasn't long until he reached the biggest building in all of the Evergreen sea kingdom. The castle.

The castle was a beautiful, open building, made of chiseled rock. Seamless pillars stretch toward the surface, with stained glass windows and sprawling coral gardens. Colored rocks made patterns through the rounded towers and columns. Hali had always idolized the royals. They were peaceful and kind, making sure that everyone in their pod was well taken care of. King Milos treated everyone like family. He let the guard live in the castle if they needed, and because of that Hali had spent a lot of time hanging out with Marni there and knew his way around.

He had only seen the king be terrifying once. A siren, their name long forgotten, had been brought to the courtyard bound in obsidian. Obsidian blocks the connection to the sea all sirens share, effectively stopping their powers and draining their energy. King Milos had asked them to apologize. To say they're sorry. He gave them a chance to avoid what came next. They didn't take it. Laughing in his face, taunting him with things that didn't make sense to anyone else but obviously affected the king. He looked terrible. His eyes were red with tears and he looked like he hadn't slept in days.

"Do it," he ordered. His eyes were cold, yet sad. The guards looked reluctant, but did as he asked, stripping the sirens of their scales. They tried to be strong, but were soon screaming and begging for mercy. Hali had only happened to be in the castle at that moment. The entire thing was supposed to be kept private. But Hali saw. He had been separated from Marni when he'd been dragged into committing mischief. No one except Marni ever knew he was there. It wasn't a sight he would ever forget.

Hali shook his head, clearing his thoughts, and kept going to his initial destination. He passed many rooms, all of them ornate and beautifully crafted, but that was not what he was looking for. He made his way to the vault. It was an almost crypt-like room with only one entrance, which was covered by golden bars made to look like kelp.

Usually, a key was needed to enter the vault. But in the last official stand of the Evergreen Sea Royal Guard, Marni was given the key by a dying officer. They were the last living members by the time it was over. When they died, Hali had taken the key and gone through the items in the vault, looking for anything that could help. While he hadn't found anything immediately useful, there was an item that would be useful now.

He swam past all the piles of gold and jewels and picked up a small wooden chest and quickly went back the way he came, pausing to lock the gate behind him. *Audra's probably worried. This took longer than I thought it would,* he thought.

When he eventually came up out of the water back into the grotto, he chuckled at what he saw. Audra had fallen asleep, slumped in an uncomfortable-looking position against one of the rocks. Hali smiled warmly, using a bit of extra magic to make pulling himself out of the water quiet. *She's so cute when she sleeps.* He brushed some hair out of her face, and she dreary blinked her eyes open. "Hey, beautiful. Have a nice nap?"

She groaned. "My back is going to be so sore tomorrow. So, what did you get?"

Hali held out the box, grinning. "I got these." Opening the box he pulled out two necklaces. They looked like a plain, simple rope with a clear orb. If they didn't come with instructions, he wouldn't have been able to use them. "These are communicators. They are normally used by the ruler and general to give orders on the battlefield. If I'm wearing one and you're wearing one then we can talk in our heads over long distances."

Audra took one of them and put it on, tucking it under her shirt. "Awesome. How do I use it?"

"Just think of talking to me and think of what you want to say," Hali instructed, putting his own one around his neck.

Audra closed her eyes in concentration. *'Hello? Hali, can you hear me?'*

'Yep! Loud and clear,' Hali responded, smiling brightly.

'This is brilliant! What's the range of these things?' Audra asked.

Hali thought. *'Eh, probably as far as we want. As long as we can think they can work. Obsidian may block them but I'm not sure.'*

Audra nodded, saying aloud, "Well, I need to head back now."

"You probably should. It's getting late," Hali told her, reluctantly.

"Yeah." She stood up slowly. Neither of them wanted to leave.

"Hey." Hali sighed. "Come back tomorrow. Bring the boys. We'll have a last party before I leave. Okay?"

Audra smiled sadly. "Okay. I'll see you tomorrow."

Audra rode home, defeated. *Hali's leaving,* she thought, her brain repeating it like a song she couldn't get out of her head. *I know it's for the best, but he's leaving. I can't help but be sad.* She put her horse away and walked to her room in silence.

"Princes Audra!" Lila greeted her as she walked in. "You've been gone for so long I was startin' to get worried. But thank heavens you are back. So! How'd it go?"

Audra tried to say something, anything, but all that came out was a sob. She crumbled. So much was going through her mind, joy, and sadness. Being told the person she loved loved her back only to know they're leaving soon.

"Oh, honey." Lila sighed, and quickly moved over to wrap her in a hug. She brushed Audra's hair and held her as she cried. "So," Lila asked cautiously after Audra had calmed down slightly. "What happened?"

Audra rubbed her eyes. "He's leaving," she answered.

"Oh, dear."

Audra sighed. "He's leaving," she repeated, "and I just found out that he likes me but he's also leaving." She stood up. "Can you help me get ready for bed, Lila?"

Lila smiled, brushing a bit of her orange hair out of her

face. "I've already laid out your night clothes. They're behind the changing screen."

Audra walked behind the screen and started getting changed. As she got undressed, she found the necklace Hali gave her. She smiled at the memory and felt more hope for the future. *He loves me. He still wants to talk to me. And it's safer for him if he leaves.* She smiled and finished getting ready for bed. And when she was in bed, just before taking off the necklace, she decided to contact him. *'Hali?'* she thought.

'Audra? Are you okay?' he responded, voice full of worry.

Audra smiled softly. *'I'm fine. I just wanted to say goodnight.'*

She could almost feel Hali's relief. In a relieved voice, he answered, *'Goodnight Audra.'*

CHAPTER 10

Audra woke up with a feeling of dread. She groaned. *Today's not going to go well, is it?* She sat up, quickly putting on her necklace. She grinned at it, the memory of yesterday flooding back into her mind. "He loves me," she whispered to herself. No one else was in the room, so she was talking to herself. *Darn it. Now I'm talking to myself. I'm not sure if that's better or worse than talking to a horse.*

There was a knock at the door, and Audra thanked the gods for a distraction from her apparent crumbling mental health. "Princess Audra! Are you up?" Lila yelled through the door.

Audra smiled and hid the necklace under her nightdress before walking to the door. "Good morning Lila."

"Good morning princess! Did you sleep well?" Lila greeted as she walked through the doorway.

Audra laughed. "I slept well. But my gut is telling me something bad is going to happen."

Lila winced, and her face twisted up like she'd eaten a lemon. "I hate to be the bearer of bad news, but the king asked to see you," she informed her sympathetically.

Audra deflated. "Yeah, that would definitely be considered bad."

Lila hummed in response as she started picking out Audra's outfit. Something relatively fancy but not overly formal. While Audra could pick out her own clothes, she tended to always wear trousers and shirts so she could fight. While that kind of clothing was fine most of the time, she would admit she had a terrible taste when it came to formal dresses. She let Lila handle formal wear.

Audra groaned and flopped on her bed. "What could he possibly want to talk about? I feel like I've done everything right so far. Well, except for kicking Ajax in the groin, but it's not like he's alive to tell him!"

Lila sputtered. "You did what?!?"

Audra shrugged. "I kneed Ajax in the balls. Honestly, he was asking for it."

Lila considered it. "True, he probably was. But honey! You can't just go around kneein' folks. Even if they ask for it." She tried to scold her, but she didn't have much of an effect because Lila was barely containing her laughter. She burst out laughing, and Audra joined her.

Audra got up, took the dress from Lila, and went behind the screen to change. The dress was dark blue, with a modest bodice and no train. It was something elegant but not fancy. Perfect for the occasion. She put it on after donning the undergarments and petticoats needed to fill out the shape. Lila helped with the lacing.

"Still," Audra continued, "the question remains as to

what my father wants."

Lila shrugged. "Well, who knows? Maybe it'll be nothin' at all and we've been worrying our pretty behinds for no reason."

Audra nodded. "I really hope you're right"

She walked through the hallways of the castle with a faux air of certainty. On the outside, she looked calm and collected. But on the inside, she was panicking. *What does he want? Is it about Ajax? Oh no, did he find out about Hali?!*

Finally, she reached her father's office door. She didn't bother knocking as she entered the room. He was expecting her anyways. He glared at her from his desk as she walked in. "I thought I told you to knock," he grumbled.

Audra cleared her throat. "Apologies. It won't happen again."

He huffed. "It better not." The king stood up slowly and walked around his desk to rest a hand on her shoulder. Audra resisted the urge to brush it off. "Audra, walk with me. There's something very important for the future we must talk about." Audra followed him through the halls of the castle. She had known he had a strong presence ever since she was young. It was something she tried to imitate. But now, walking with him, she could see he emanated fear and not respect. People in the halls scurried to get out of his way, and some even cowered. Audra didn't like it. If you were leading people, they should trust you. They shouldn't fear you.

He led her to one of the highest windows in the castle. It was in a secluded tower and had a nice view of the port. He stopped there, turning so the two were face to face. "When you look out this window," he started, "what do you see?"

Audra took a look. She could see the ships in the harbor, the market just getting ready to open, and people starting their day. "The port. And the city. And all the people who call it home," she answered.

Her father nodded. "Yes. It is our kingdom. Our family's legacy. Our ancestors have worked hard to create a society free of pests. Centuries of hard work have led to this."

Audra cocked her head. "I don't think I understand. Father, what are you talking about?"

He laughed. *Laughed.* Audra paled. *Nothing good can come out of this,* she thought.

"This," he gestured vaguely at the town, "is something completely beyond your comprehension. We are coming to the final step in the master plan. This plan is why I originally chose Ajax as the best possible future king. He shared my ideals, and his father has been a great asset in our fight."

Audra hummed in acknowledgment. "What about Mel and Cassius? From my experience, they would be more than capable as kings."

He shook his head. "They are... adequate, I suppose. But not what I'm looking for in a king. They wouldn't be devoted to the mission. Ajax, on the other hand, the Andelion royal family had provided aid before. He would be willing to uphold our paradise. His passing was a tragedy," he explained, side-eyeing Audra pointedly at the mention of Ajax's passing.

She looked away. "It was, I agree." That was all she said.

"Audra," he started in a tone you would use to scold a child, "I'm aware that you had a hand in Ajax's death."

Audra froze, and her face filled with fear for a moment before she sculpted it back to a neutral expression. "I'm not sure what you mean," she tried, cursing her slight stutter.

"Do not think me a fool!" he spat. Sighing, he pinched the bridge of his nose. "I'm aware you had a part in his murder. Now, for the sake of keeping peace with Andelion as well as maintaining our public image..."

Audra resisted the urge to snort. *What public image? The people don't like you.*

"I will not take action against you," he finished.

"If what you're implying is true," she started cautiously, "then why even tell me?"

He let out a tired sigh. "To remind you of your duty. You have an obligation to be loyal to your kingdom and the paradise our ancestors have created." He went quiet for a minute, staring out the window in contemplative silence. "Just know this. You are on thin ice. I will forgive this little slip-up, but I will not forget it." With those final words, he walked past her and out of the tower, leaving Audra alone with her thoughts.

What just happened? she thought. Apparently, her brain decided to freeze instead of trying to process what that meant. Before she had time to unfreeze her brain, she was interrupted by the sound of quick footsteps. On guard, Audra got into a defensive position. "Who's there?!"

"Whoa!" a familiar voice called out. "It's just me."

Audra lowered her fists. "Mel? What are you

doing here?"

The boy in question was standing at the top of the stairs, hands held up to show he wasn't attacking. His orange hair looked more messy than normal, and his light brown pants had grass stains on the knees. He dropped his hands and fell back into a more normal stance. "I saw you and your father come up here. I just wanted to make sure you were alright."

Audra sighed, and Mel made his way over to sit on one of the boxes in the room. She started pacing. "I'm fine, but I just had a very strange conversation."

"What was it about?" he asked.

"Well, the most important thing is that he knows I had a part in Ajax's death."

"Oh," Mel said, stunned. "That's bad. Yeah. That's definitely not good."

Audra paused her pacing to nod and continued, "And that's not even the weird part! He said he's not going to do anything about it!"

Mel's eyes widened in alarm. "Really?"

"Really."

"Are you sure?"

"Yeah."

Mel paused. "Huh. He doesn't seem like the type of person to do that."

Audra shook her head. "He's not. Which makes all of this ten times as weird."

He shrugged. "Well, look on the bright side! At least you don't have to worry about getting in trouble for that."

"I guess you're right." Audra shrugged. "But, other things he said aren't lining up."

Mel cocked his head to the side. He looked a bit childish, with wide eyes and sitting cross-legged. "Like what? Maybe I can help."

"It was weird. Like he was talking about something I should know but don't. He was talking about our legacy and our ancestors and how he has almost created a utopia. He told me to look out the window and see our greatest creation," Audra explained.

"Well then." Mel jumped from his seat. "Let's take a look. Maybe he means literally?"

So she did. Audra looked out the window again. Really looked. Her brain raced to catalog everything she could see. The buildings. The ocean. The ships. The people.

The people.

It's just humans.

"Oh no."

CHAPTER 11

Marni's cave was just as empty and dark as she had left it. It didn't feel right. Marni was so loud and bright. And here was so silent. They would hate it.

Marni's trident was still embedded in the floor. Hali floated up to it, reaching out to brush silt from its handle and run her hands along the grooves. She knew every mark on that trident. Every imperfection had a story to go with it. Marni loved to tell them, and Hali loved to listen. When they ran out of stories to tell, Hali would ask to hear old ones. Marni never minded repeating themselves. Their trident was their pride and joy after all. At this point, Hali could probably tell each story herself, able to recite each and every one of them from memory.

She didn't tell them out loud. They wouldn't sound right in her voice instead of Marni's.

"Hey, Marni," she said into the still water, whispering for only the ghost of her friend to hear. The ocean swallowed the sound whole. The world did not deserve her grief, and the ocean would make sure it stayed silent to the rest. "Guess what? I have a way out."

She laughed brokenly and slid down so her tail could curl around the trident. "Marni, I'm sorry. I'm leaving. I hired someone to take me away from here. I'm sorry. You were supposed to come with me. I can't take you with me."

Purple, oozing tears slid down her cheeks. A sob made its way out her throat. The skulls on the walls seemed to be staring at her. Every one of them. She had never counted exactly how many there were, she had never bothered. It had always made her a bit uneasy to hear Marni talk about them. She wished she could hear Marni talk about them now. The skulls looked at her with pity in their nonexistent eyes. She didn't like it, not at all.

"Look at me, Marni. I'm still the crybaby you always said I was," she said, somewhere between a laugh and a sob. The skull's gaze turned disapproving, and Hali flinched. She swam up and held on to the trident one last time. "What I'm trying to say is goodbye, Marni. I won't forget you."

She let go and swam out of the cave. She rolled the rock at the entrance forward, sealing it forever.

It was sunset when Hali made her way back to The Swan and Dolphin. The sky was a mix of orange and pink clouds, colored by the sun hiding behind them. It looked like a watercolor painting. Hali took it as a sign of good things to come.

Audra had helped Hali plan a route through the back alleys of the city. It was safer than being so out in the open, especially at night when people were heading home from their jobs. Hali did miss the sounds of people, though. They were muffled and distant from where she was. The alleys were smaller as well, and darker. The shadows stretched down the street.

Hali would miss Carnelian. She hadn't been up on land for long, but it was all she had ever known. How would other kingdoms look? How would they sound? Would the streets feel the same under her feet, made of cold cobblestone? Would the houses be made of something entirely different? She didn't know. She didn't even know what kingdom she would end up near, having not planned to go any farther than 'out.' The Shining Sea Pod had offered to take her in. Maybe she would take them up on it. She'd have to get to know them better first. If she did join them, she would be by Cassius. That would be nice.

Cassius. And Mel, and Audra! She would miss them. For the first time in so long she had friends! She was in love, she had fallen hard and fast. Miracle of all miracles, her love was requited. It was new and scary, but it was theirs. Her and Audra's.

She was never going to see Audra again, was she? Or, if she did, it wouldn't be for a long time. What they had now was so good! And they didn't even have time to try and make it work. They didn't have time to make it stronger.

Why couldn't she stay? What was stopping her? Sure, it would be dangerous and she might die, but it would be worth it. She could stay.

So absorbed in her thoughts, she didn't even notice she had reached The Swan and Dolphin until the sounds of the pub were caught by her webbed ears. Hali took a deep breath and buried any thoughts of staying deep down. Those dreams of a happy life with her friends and love would do her no good now. It was too late to back out. She had already opened the door.

The Swan and Dolphin was packed, just like it had been last time. There were more sailors than last time, she noticed. *It's probably because the princes are here.* It was good for her that it was busy. People were less likely to notice two suspicious individuals leaving if there were a lot of things happening around them.

The man from before was sitting in one of the back booths, cloak pulled over his head and looking just as ominous as before. Hali held the hood of her cape as she pushed her way through the crowd. She wasn't going to let it fall off this time.

"Did you bring the tickets?" he asked her while she sat down. She nodded. "Good. Would have been a shame if you had lost them. I spent my hard-earned money to get them, you know?"

She glared at him out of the corner of her eye. "Take me to the ship," she demanded.

He sighed and stood up. "Come along then."

She followed him back through the hoard of people and out the door. They took the main roads this time. He was a fast walker, and with Hali's lackluster walking skills, she struggled to keep up.

"What's taking so long?!" he barked. Hali flinched and pulled her hood further down when people glanced over.

"I can't walk very well," she answered.

He rolled his eyes and stomped back over to her,

grabbing her roughly by the arm. His fingernails dug into the patch of scales there and she barely restrained herself from crying out. "Oh don't cry now. The hard part is just beginning. If you can't walk, I'll just pull you along."

Hali stumbled to keep up with him, her arm burning in pain and clouding her vision. Something was wrong. She just couldn't place what. Not when her mind was focused on keeping her feet moving and herself from screaming.

He kept muttering as they walked, and it took Hali a few seconds to make out what he was saying. "They're waiting for us. We can't be late. We wouldn't be late if this stupid girl knew how to walk." She didn't like it one bit.

He veered into a side alley, and suddenly Hali realized why everything felt wrong. They weren't heading toward the ocean. "Where are you taking me?" she asked, fear clear in her voice.

"To the ship," was all he answered.

She shook her head. "No, we aren't headed to the ship. Where are you going?"

"Listen, kid," he growled at her. "I was trying to let you down easy, but you just had to start asking questions."

"Where are you taking me?" she demanded, giving him her best glare. She tried to squirm her way out of his grip, but every little movement agitated her scales and sent waves of pain through her.

"I'm taking you to the guards," he sneered. Hali gasped. She started squirming more, but he just tightened his grip. "They promised to pay me double for turning in the last siren. It's just money, kid. Nothing personal." She opened her mouth to scream. It was the last thing she could do. A hand blacked her mouth, covering her mouth and nose. She couldn't breath. "If you're lucky," he continued as she clawed at his hand, drawing blood, "they'll kill you in your sleep."

Black spots appeared in her vision. "*Audra!*" she screamed into the mental connection before everything went black.

"*Audra!*"

Audra sat bolt upright in bed, Hali's pained voice still ringing in her head. She sounded panicked and scared. "*Hali?*" she called out through their mental connection. "*Hali? Please answer. Are you alright?*" There was no reply. "*Hali! Please!*" she called desperately. The line was still silent.

Audra got out of bed and changed into some trousers and a shirt before starting to pace her room. *What happened? Is Hali okay? Is Hali dead? Please tell me she's not dead.* Audra thought. She rubbed her hands together, worry oozing off her in waves.

A knock on the door interrupted her pacing. "Are you awake, milady?" Audra smiled in relief. Lila.

"Yes, I am. Come in," she answered. Lila opened the door, stepping inside with a fake smile plastered on her face. Audra could tell. Her eyes still looked solemn. "Lila? What's wrong?" she asked.

Lila stiffened. "It's nothin', milady," she answered, avoiding eye contact.

"It clearly isn't," Audra shot back. "Lila, if there's

something wrong I want to know. Maybe I can help."

Lila sighed. "It's about why I'm here. Your father has summoned you." Audra's eyes widened. "But that's not it. I saw it on my way here. They were draggin' a siren to the dungeons."

Audra stepped back. *Hali's been caught?* she questioned. Audra looked back to Lila. "Are you sure it was a siren?" she asked.

Lila nodded solemnly. "I'm positive."

Audra cursed. That would explain why Hali was so panicked about their mind connection. She pushed the thought down, looking at Lila. "Why are you not happy about this?" she asked.

Lila looked down, not making eye contact. "Forgive me, milady. But I do not agree that sirens are evil. I believe they are like humans. With equal capacity for good and evil. Seein' them killed... it's just wrong."

Audra nodded. "Don't tell anyone about this, but I feel the same way. And that's why I'm going to try and stop this." Lila smiled, and Audra walked out the door with determination.

The king was, as usual, waiting for her in his office. This time, however, he was looking out the large window behind his desk, facing away from her. "You didn't knock. Again," he commented.

"What did you call me here for, Father? It's late and I was preparing for bed." A bit of sass crept into her voice.

"This won't take long. I would merely like to inform you that the siren has been captured," he explained.

"Oh," Audra responded, not sure what else to say. She already knew Hali was captured. There were things she wanted to say, of course. She wanted to yell. To scream and demand he let her go. But that would only make the situation worse. She wasn't foolish. He had the power in this situation.

"In a few days, we can put your little lapse of judgment behind us," he continued.

Audra paused. "Lapse of judgment?"

"I told you I'm not a fool. Despite your best efforts, it's clear that a siren was involved in your murder plot against Prince Ajax. She has been dealt with. Once she is gone we can forget about your minor betrayal."

"You consider murder minor?" she asked.

He laughed. "Our kingdom is built on blood rightfully spilled. One soul is merely a scratch on our legacy."

"That doesn't make it any better. All life is important," she argued.

He sighed. "It doesn't matter anyway. That beast is special to you, isn't it?"

"No," she lied, though she knew there wasn't much of a point.

"You think you're good at lying, but I've known you all your life. You have the same tells as your mother. Your ears twitch when you lie. Your ears were moving quite a lot when you told me about Prince Ajax's death. And you even defend sirens. I can see right through you."

Audra's shoulders dropped. "If you choose to do this I will not stand by your side."

"Oh, you will," the mad king stated. "If you don't want

that siren to be hurt, then you will." That made Audra hesitate. "You will do what I say. If you don't, I will not hesitate to hurt the siren. You wouldn't want it to be tortured, would you? I'll tell you how I'd start. Pulling out a siren scale is the worst way to hurt them. From what I've heard, they'll be in complete agony if they even lose one. So, know this. if you disobey me, if you do anything to try and stop this, I will pull all of its scales. So, if you really care for it, you'll go back to your room without saying a thing. You're dismissed."

Audra grit her teeth and walked out. This wasn't the plan. Hali was supposed to be safe. And now, she can't even help her without risking getting her hurt. She walked back into her room and collapsed on her chair, letting a few tears fall. 'Hali?' she tried. No response.

There was a knock at the door. Audra jumped out of her chair and practically bolted to open the door. On the other side stood Lila. "Princess? Are you alright?"

Despite her desperate attempts to hold them in, she felt tears fall down her cheeks. Lila closed the door and quickly led her over to the bed, comfortingly rubbing her shoulder. "Lila, can you keep a secret?" she asked through sobs.

"Of course. I always will," Lila answered. That was all the encouragement Audra needed.

"The person I love. The one I told you about? It's her. It's the siren they brought in earlier." She saw Lila draw in a breath but otherwise not say anything. "I don't know how to help her. If my father finds out, he'll hurt her even more. I can't risk that." Audra suddenly remembered what Henry had told her. "Lila, we need Warren's luck."

It was like a switch was flipped. Lila smiled. "So, someone gave you the code word. Really, it was about time." She stood up and pulled on one of the candle holders in her room. Audra's mouth dropped to the floor as a hidden door opened. Lila started to walk down the hallway. "Follow me."

Audra considered her options. This was very suspicious. How she hadn't even known there was a secret passage here was the strangest part. She shouldn't trust this. But on the other hand, she knew Lila. Lila was loyal. She was always there when Audra needed her. And, maybe, wherever Lila was taking her would help. So, she stood up and followed Lila through the passageway.

The inside was narrow, but not so small it was hard to walk in. Lila had lit a torch and was using that to lead the way. "Lila?"

"Yes, milady?"

"What is this place?" Audra asked.

"These are the old servant tunnels. They haven't been used in a long time, so we've taken them over," Lila answered.

"Who's we?"

Lila smiled at her. "You'll see."

Audra couldn't tell how long they'd been walking or where they were, but Lila obviously did. She moved around the maze of stairs and passageways as if it was second nature. They passed many doors, and Audra wondered how she had never known this was here. The tunnels seemed to stretch on for miles. The only light came from Lila's torch, making shadows dance across the walls. After a while, Lila stopped in front of a door. This door was different than the others. It looked new, and the symbol of a war room, a sword, and shield was painted on the door in red paint.

Lila turned to face her. "Before we go in, I want you to swear to me you won't tell anyone about this. And that means anyone. I'm takin' a huge risk by bringing you here."

Audra nodded. "I swear I won't."

Lila smiled. "Alright." Lila opened the door, and Audra stepped into the room. They were in a large cavern, which opened out to the sea. Around a small table, a group of people stood. Audra recognized some of them. They were merchants or servants in the castle, and there were even a few knights! Piles of weapons, armor, and other supplies lined the walls.

"What's all this? Who are you guys?"

Lila laughed. "Princess Audra, meet the revolution."

Chapter 12

Audra was shocked. Questions raced through her head. *A revolution? And they had full access to the castle? Why didn't they do something sooner? Better question, why did they ask me to join?* Her confusion must have shown on her face, as she heard a low chuckle from one of the others in the room.

"A little surprised, aren't we? Don't worry so much. We don't mean any harm. Well, to you at least." A muscled man with orange hair said. It took Audra a minute to recognize him.

"Sir Warner!" She smiled. "It's been a while."

The man, Sir Warner, laughed. "Two years isn't all that long. And there's no need to call me a sir. Not yet at least. I'm not technically a knight."

Audra scoffed. "You're one of the strongest and most noble men I've ever met. You're more of a knight than a lot of the other knights can ever dream of being. She saw a few of the other knights in the room, the noble ones, perk their heads up. "No offense," she added quickly.

Audra scanned the room, trying to see who was there. Doing a quick head count, she saw there were twenty people, not counting herself and Lila. Four of them were the knights she had knighted two years ago after they helped her when she got captured by bandits in the mountains. Another three were her father's knights. There were four servants and four merchants. There were three nobles she recognized as Lady Willow, Lord Balloren, and Lord Andre. She was glad it was those three. She didn't know them too well, but they seemed like the least snotty of the nobles. And the greatest surprise of all, Mel and Cassius were standing at the table.

"*Cass!?*" She screamed.

Cassius turned around. "Hello, Audra. Honestly, I'm not surprised to see you here."

Mel ran towards her and wrapped her in a hug. "Audra! I heard about what happened with Hali. I'm so, so sorry. We'll make sure she's okay.

"I- Uh... What... *Huh?!?*" she stuttered. "What are you of all people doing in a revolutionary group?"

Cassius's lips quirked up in that funny half-smile Audra had figured out meant that he was amused. "Well, my original purpose for coming here was to kill both you and your father for the massacre of the Evergreen Sea Pod." Audra flinched. "But," he continued, "thanks to your brilliant siren partner defending you from the ruler of the Shining Sea Pod, The plan has been changed. The goal now is to overthrow your father."

Mel nodded. "Yep! Luckily, we didn't have to do a lot of the work. We just found the people who had already started the work."

"What do you mean?"

It was at that moment that Sir Warner finally noticed

Lila, who had been hanging in the back of the room. "Ah! General Lila! Come over here! We have to discuss battle plans!"

Lila blushed. "I'm not a general, Warner. There's no need to go callin' me that."

Warner shrugged. "You're as much a general as I am a knight."

"Lila?" Audra asked, shocked. "What's going on?"

Both adults turned to her. Lila smiled sadly. "I'm sorry for keeping this from you, darlin. The truth is, I've been leading a revolution. I just hate the way your father runs things. I hate seeing how he makes you sad."

Lila? A revolutionary? I never would have guessed, Audra thought. She was still reeling, but when things get strange she tends to fall back on logic. And right now logic was telling her these people could help. "I would like to work with you. Especially if Hali's safety is a priority. My father's ways are terrible, and I should have done something sooner."

"Thank you." Lila patted her arm, and they all walked over to the planning table. Audra gave polite nods to the other people at the table before getting to work.

"Now, our plan was originally going to be this: The majority of our forces will storm the front gate with the help of the knights working with us. The rest of our forces will hide in the passageways to block off any potential exits. We would then force our way into the throne room, where Lady Willow, Lord Balloren, and Lord Andre would have lured him. Once there I will tell him to surrender his crown to you or die." Sir Warner moved to point at another map, this one of the entire islands with the small military outposts marked. "While this is happening, some of our forces from other parts of the island will lead similar attacks on the army posts. The one problem is the wall. We don't have a way to take it down. There are too many guards and no way to get on top of it. We've decided that we will regain control of the wall after taking over the throne."

"I have a way," Cassius started. "Outside the wall, armies from the Shining Sea Pod are stationed. They're waiting for a command to attack."

Warner nodded. "Righty-o. I'll add that."

Lila then took over the explanation. "But we now have a new problem. The siren."

"Hali," Audra interrupted.

Sir Warner nodded. "Right. Hali. Well, with Hali in the dungeons, we have a new variable to consider. The King could use them as a hostage in this situation."

"He already is," Audra stated. "He's holding her safety over my head. He'll torture her if I don't do what he says. And I don't doubt he will. He sounded insane when I talked to him earlier."

"I can see what I can do," Lila butted in. "The cook was discussin' who would have to go give Hali food. If I can convince her to have that be me, I can find out how they are keepin' her. How many guards there are, what cell she's in, and if there's any secret opening nearby."

Audra nodded. "Thank you, Lila. That would be wonderful. I don't think I'll be allowed anywhere near her."

"I take it this Hali is important to you?" Sir

Warner questioned.

Audra smiled. "Yes. She's very important to me. I'd do anything to keep her safe."

"Good." He then turned his attention back to the maps on the table. "So, her safety is a priority to you. Based on your face, I'd say it's the first priority. So, I will make that a high priority."

Audra was relieved. "Thank you."

He simply nodded. "Well, I believe most of our plans will stay the same. Based on what information Lila gets we can decide what to do later. I think it would be wise to send a small group down to rescue Hali."

"I think Audra, Cassius, and I should be on the team to rescue Hali," Mel announced. "It would be better if she had people she trusted."

Lila nodded. "Good. I trust you'll be able to handle yourselves. I suggest we meet again tomorrow. I'll see you all then."

"Why does she call you a knight?" Lila asked after another servant had escorted Audra and the other royals off to bed. Most had turned in for the evening, leaving Lila and Warner alone in the revolutionary's cave. They sat at the table, going over the map of the throne room one last time.

Warner paused. "It's a long story, and not all that interesting, really."

Warner was a gentleman, and real easy on the eyes Lila had to admit. With a big red beard and his even bigger muscles, any gal would be lucky to have him. His loose hanging tunic made the view even better as it showed off his fine, hairy chest.

"Well, you can tell me, can't you?" Lila prodded. She needed to know! Yes, Audra was respectful, the darlin' that she was. But she doesn't just randomly give someone a title! "Please, Warner, I'm curious. Indulge me."

He laughed. "Alright. The princess was taking a trip through one of the mountain passes, alone."

She gasped. "That's a horrible idea! What was she thinking?"

"I don't know." Warner shrugged. "All I know is that all of this happened after her mother died, so her running off probably had something to do with that."

"She would have been what, eight?"

"Nine. And tiny. I have no idea how she got a horse, but she did and used it to ride up into the mountains. As expected, she was attacked by bandits. I was on my way down the mountain to go into town, but I saw a kid getting attacked and I couldn't walk away." His voice was soft and distant as he reminisced. He wasn't bragging or boasting. Lila added *humble* to the mental list she had going of reasons she liked him.

He continued. "She insisted she knight me for my service to the kingdom. I didn't realize she was the princess, so I let her. I told her it was now my duty to walk her home. And then she took me too the castle. I thought that maybe one of her parents work there. I just didn't think it would be the king!"

Lila laughed. "She did try to tell you."

"She did! I just didn't believe it would be true." His

face turned somber. "He didn't even thank me, you know."

"Who?"

"The king. Her father. She could have died, and he didn't even thank me for saving her. Gods, he didn't even come to check on her until at least the next day, after I had left. So many servants and knights came flooding to the medical wing to make sure she was alright, but him?" He shook his head. "He didn't. And I know he was told she was there. I asked."

"Bastard, bless his heart," Lila mumbled.

Warner nodded in agreement. "He'll be gone soon enough. I've seen Audra a few times after that, but never for very long. I'm excited to work with her."

"I am too, but I was hopin' she wouldn't've needed to be brought into all of this." She sighed. "I had a plan and everything. I'd've made some of the girls, the ones who can't fight you know? They would have taken her to the meadow."

"The one at the base of the mountain?" he asked.

"That's the one I'm talking about! That one! You can't see the water from there. Or the castle. She wouldn't have had to know any of this was happening until much later. Of course, things change."

"The siren."

"And the princes. I like them fine, but they came at just the wrong time and started poking their heads all up in our business! Now, I'm glad Audra has friends. The girl needed some, besides myself of course. I'm also not mad she fell in love."

Warner smiled. "One of these days, we'll get to meet

the one who stole her heart."

Lila frowned. "If the gods allow it. I'm hoping, but hope can only get us so far."

"You're right. Skill and planning will have to take us the rest of the way there."

Both of them looked back down at the maps. Some were new, having been drawn when the wall went up. Simple maps of the kingdom with important spots marked. Others were older, those had to have been stolen. They detailed outpost locations, army movements, and other things not known to the public. The final maps were crumbling. They had been drawn long, LONG ago. Back when the castle had first been constructed. Someone who was forgotten to time had thought to make a map of the servant tunnels. Every secret passageway and hidden room was there.

"It's a miracle," Lila commented.

"What is?"

"That someone who could fix our problems came along at the perfect moment."

Warner paused. "The princes or the sirens?"

"Both," Lila answered. Warner's gaze flicked to the floor, full of anger for a minute. And then it was gone as he looked back up at her. "Do you trust them?" she asked.

He considered it. "Enough. I think they'll get the job done."

"Then what's the problem?" she prodded.

He looked at the water in the cave. The light from their candle reflected on the water, making the tiny waves sparkle. A small sliver of moonlight filtered in from the entrance. "This is our kingdom," he eventually said. "If we're going to take it back, we should be the ones to do it."

"Why?"

"It's a matter of honor. Are we really fit to run this kingdom if we had to rely on help to take it?"

Lila pondered this. "Well, there's no changin' it now. We need them."

"You're right," Warner conceded. "There's no changing anything now."

CHAPTER 13

It's cold. That was the first coherent thought Hali had when she drifted back into consciousness. Cautiously, she opened her eyes only to find herself in a dark cell. She looked around, not having enough energy to form any kind of panic. The cell was made out of dark gray bricks and had no windows. One side, the one she was facing, was completely made of obsidian bars that led out into a dimly lit hallway.

She pulled herself up, making her way to the bars despite her body's protests. Everything ached. She was stopped by a sharp pull on her wrists. Looking down, she found obsidian cuffs attached to the wall behind her.

Welp, she thought. *That's not good.*

Her head was pounding. It was hard to focus on anything. The pain in her side had subsided, but that might just be the fact that every muscle in her body felt sore and she had just gone numb to it. She didn't have many options. The obsidian cuffs were blocking her magic, otherwise, she would use that. But seeing as that wasn't an option, she knew she was going to die.

And wasn't that a strange thought? She had spent so long fearing death, but now that it was inevitable she barely felt affected. Hali felt empty. Like something was missing. Something important. She knew what it was. Her family. Her friends. When she died, she would most likely get to see them again. And that thought comforted her. At least she could go out saying she tried instead of just giving up.

She collapsed on the floor, not having the energy to do much more. She was about to give in to the comforting thought of sleep when she heard something. *"Hali?"* Audra. Of course. The void in Hali's heart filled just a little from hearing her voice. Even if it was only in her head. There was Audra to live for. If she couldn't at least try to stay alive for herself she would try for Audra.

"Are you a siren? Because you have the most enchanting voice I have ever heard." she flirted.

Hali could almost feel the relief Audra felt through their mental connection. *"Hali! One, that was such a terrible pickup line I don't even know where to start. Second, thank the gods you're alright!"*

Hali chuckled. *"One, you know you love it. Two, I'm as fine as I can be."*

"Oh, gods. Are you hurt? Do you feel alright?" Audra asked with concern.

"If having my entire body be sore and my head throbbing while feeling so exhausted I really just want to sleep alright then yeah I'm alright," she responded.

"I'm sorry," Audra said guiltily.

Hali was confused. *"What for? You didn't do anything."*

"That's exactly the problem!" Audra answered. "I didn't protect you."

Hali smiled sadly. "If you're blaming yourself for me getting captured, then you'd better stop. It wasn't, and never will be, your fault. You weren't there."

"I know... but I should have been. I should have come with you. Or at least done more to make sure you were safe. Gods, I should have just smuggled you onto the royal ship and gotten you out of here myself." Audra stated bitterly.

Hali softened. "Don't. Don't go down that eel hole. If you keep blaming yourself you won't ever be able to stop. Trust me. I've been there. Listen to me. Are you listening to me?"

There was a short pause before Audra cursed and then said a quick, "Yes."

"Good. I need you to trust me. I don't blame you. I will never blame you. The only reason I got caught was my own foolishness. No fault of yours. Got that?"

"Yeah. I'll try not to blame myself. But it's hard," Audra responded.

"I know." The two then fell into a tense silence. "So," Hali started cautiously. "What was that pause earlier?"

"Oh that. Heh." Audra chuckled awkwardly. "I nodded and then realized you can't actually see me.'"

Hali laughed, "So, not to be a downer or anything but why am I not dead?"

After a minute Audra spoke. "Honestly? I'm not really sure. I spoke with him earlier, but he made it sound like he was going to kill you, but not immediately. He knows we were working together. He's smarter than I give him credit for, *apparently. But he said that if I tried to stop him from killing you he would rip out your scales."*

Hali paled at the thought of getting a scale ripped off.

"I can feel your fear," Audra informed her, startling Hali out of her reverie. *"It really is bad, getting your scales pulled out. Isn't it?"*

"Yes. It's the worst form of torture imaginable," Hali responded. *"Audra? I'm scared."*

"I understand. I would be too. Honestly, I'm scared for you. It's alright to be scared. And this will all be over soon. I'll try my hardest. I have a plan to get you out of there and get my father off the throne. But you've just got to hold on until then," Audra reassured her. Her voice was soft.

Hali smiled. *"I'll try."*

It was all there, and Audra would have found it ages ago if she had gotten the courage to look. Sir Warner had joined her in searching through the books in her father's study, and a servant she wasn't familiar with but vowed to learn the name of was keeping watch outside.

Her family had been committing genocide for ages. It started with her great-grandfather, who wanted to set up guard outposts in the mountains. The avians didn't like that, so he started hunting them. It wasn't noticed too much by the people because avians didn't come down to the city often. But it was still recorded, talked about as if it was some great victory.

Much more discreetly, and much more recently, was her grandfather. He had every hive in the kingdom assassinated. A series of freak accidents is what the people thought. It wasn't like there were very many hives in the kingdom, to begin with.

Her father, well, that was a story she knew by heart. She was living it, after all.

She sank down into her father's chair. "Gods… I didn't know."

"No one knew. Or, well, very few people knew, I guess," Sir Warner assured her.

"I should have known. It's my family history."

"How could you? You were never told." He paused. "You weren't told, were you?"

"I wasn't."

"Ah."

She flipped through the books again, not reading a thing. She just needed to see it so she knew it was there. They didn't say anything for a minute. It was a lot to process, after all.

"Do you think my mom knew?" she finally asked.

Sir Warner thought. "Do you think your father would have told her?"

Audra paused and thought about everything she knew of her father. "She didn't know. She wouldn't have married him if she did.If there was anything he could do to help ease that danger, he would do it. Besides, he wouldn't have told her anyway. Probably didn't think she was strong enough to help."

Sir Warner grabbed the book from her. It was probably for the best that she didn't have it anyway. She would have just kept reading it over and over again. Like picking open a scab on a still-healing wound. "Gods..." he muttered. "This whole thing is a mess."

"Do you know what I just realized?" Audra asked.

He hummed and set the book down out of her reach. She didn't make any kind of move to stop him. "No. I don't."

"If he had told me, since the beginning, that this..." She gestured to the book. "Was our family's pride and joy, I would have agreed with him."

Sir Warner paused. "What?"

"I always wanted to please him," she spit out. "More than anything, especially as a kid. Mother? She was easy. She would love me no matter what I did for the simple fact that I was her child. But Father? That's a whole different story. I was never good enough for him. Never! It was always 'I expect better from you, Audra' or 'You've disappointed me, Audra.' Even worse, I can't remember any time I have heard him say he loves me that wasn't him trying to impress friends. If he had told me, when I was little, that if I killed the sirens I would make him proud and he would love me? I would have been the one to lead the charge."

"That can't be true."

"It can. Sure, my mother would have been opposed to it. But she would have been long dead by then. If he had just talked to me and showed he was there for me when I needed him the most, he could have fed the small spark of anger I had at the sirens into something much, much bigger. Instead, his coldness killed it and only made me angry at him." Audra laughed bitterly, though it was a sound closer to a sob. "I hate to admit it, but I know myself. And I know him. I'm just like him, deep down. I'm my father's daughter, after all."

"Stop," Sir Warner interrupted. His voice was cold and serious in a way Audra had never heard from the usually kind and goofy man. It made her stop speaking and listen. "Don't. You're not like him, at least in the ways that matter."

"You don't know him like I do," she shot back.

"No, maybe not. But I know what you're feeling, and as someone older and wiser I need to tell you that you're wrong." He took a deep breath and sank into the chair across from Audra. The chair she usually sat on whenever she was in this office. It felt weird, to be sitting in her father's usual spot. She did understand why her father liked this spot though. The angle made you feel like you had power over whoever was across from you.

Sir Warner sighed. "My parents," he started slowly, "were bandits in the mountains."

Audra gasped. "Really? But isn't your whole mission to end crime in the mountains?"

He nodded. "Yes, it is. And that's for a reason. I've seen what crime is like, seen what it can do to a person. That's why I'm trying to stop it. Audra, we can be like our parents. You can have that same drive, and ambition, and anger that he does. That's a good thing to have, actually. I really don't want to say anything good about your father but he is strong. That's not what matters though. It's what you do with those traits," he told her.

Audra nodded and felt one lone tear drip down her face. It's strange what a few words can do, especially if you've been waiting to hear them. "I understand," she whispered.

"Your father has chosen to be a terrible person. He has chosen to hurt so many people. But that's his choice, not yours. You do have a choice, Audra. And just the fact that you feel guilty about what could have been means you chose correctly. You and me? We are who we are in spite of who we were created by."

Audra pondered all of this. "You're very wise, Sir Warner."

He chuckled. "I thought I told you not to call me Sir. I'm not a knight."

She shrugged. "But you will be. Once we win and I'm queen."

Sir Warner smiled. "Then I'll look forward to it."

Mel was glad no one knew who he was right now. It would make sneaking out of the palace a lot harder if he was a recognizable figure. He still wore the hood of his cloak up just in case, but if anyone saw his face it wouldn't matter. He blended in easily here. He wasn't a prince, as much as his title said otherwise. But that's all it was. A title. Back home it was barely something people thought about. He was just another average person surrounded by even more average people. Other kingdoms, he'd come to realize, had a lot more of a division based on social class. Not like Cerulean.

It was nighttime in the city, which really just hammered home the fact that there was something missing from the town. A distinct lack of any type of magic. With so many hives and fairies in Cerulean, not seeing them here was startling.

He made it to his destination, a small building close to the docks named The Rhododendron Inn. It was a three-story building with a wood frame and a thatched roof. The lights were off in most of the upstairs windows, but a warm golden glow showed through the 1st-floor windows, inviting him in. He pushed open the door slowly and was immediately hit by the smell of alcohol. He scrunched up his nose and pushed through.

It was like a party inside, with the booths filled with sailors who had been drinking for quite a few hours at this point. There was dancing, laughing, and the telling of stories happening anywhere he looked. Mel loved it.

He took off his hood, and immediately there was a call of "Prince Mel!" From the corner of the room. Sure enough, there was his crew. Sitting around one giant round table with their blue sashes around their arms. A few had yellow sashes as well, and even some red ones. It was nice to know his people got along well with the people from his friend's kingdoms.

Tomy, one of the older sailors, waved at him. "Mel! Come join us! They have great mead here!" which was followed by a chorus of agreement from the rest of the table.

Mel laughed. "Guys, you know I don't like alcohol."

Amina, a younger sailor who was the closest to his age on the crew, patted the seat next to her. "Then just sit with us for a while. It's been a couple days since we've seen you! We want to know everything."

Mel considered it. "I'll stay." The group cheered as he sat down. "But only for a little while." They groaned.

"Oh come on! What's the rush?" Tomy asked.

Gregory, one of the more strict members of the crew, piped up. "Because he's supposed to be staying at the castle. What are you doing down here, anyway?"

"I'm here for important business, actually. I need to talk to Imogene. It's important, but it can wait a couple of minutes," Mel answered.

Amina nodded. "Ah, she hasn't been coming down often. Says she's not feeling well, but that feels like an excuse. See if you can find out what's up, yeah?"

Mel frowned. "I'll ask, but it isn't that out of character for Imogene not to come to the bar. You know she doesn't like to party all that much."

"You're right, but still. She always at least comes down to eat her meal and then go back up. Something seems off, though. I wonder what."

"Let's not ponder on that now!" Tomy interrupted. "Tell us, how's Cassius?"

"Prince Cassius," one of the sailors from Andelion corrected. They were very big on using the proper titles for their royals. When he'd asked why, they had told him it was a sign of respect in Andelion. In Cerulean, it was more respectful not to use proper titles.

"Right right. How's Prince Cassius doing? You two get up to anything fun?"

Mel blushed. "Well, he's good. A bit stressed with all of this, but good. Oh! And I made a new friend!"

"Really, who?" Gregory asked.

"Princess Audra! She's really nice, actually."

"Oh? I wasn't expecting that," Tomy pointed out.

One of the red sailors glared. "Are you bad mouthing our princess?"

"No no!" Tomy tried to backtrack. It wasn't working. The Carnelian sailors were just getting angrier and angrier. "I was just…."

"I'm going to go talk to Imogene now!" Mel stood up and booked it over to the stairs. It felt like then was a good time to leave, and he was proven right as just a few seconds later he heard the sounds of a bar fight breaking out. He knew that there wasn't actually that much animosity between the people at the table, they had just been looking for a fight. *Sailors,* he thought.

It didn't take him long to find Imogene's room. The Rhododendron Inn grouped sailors by kingdom of origin to avoid skrimishes and inter-kingdom fights. It was a system that worked, for the most part. Fights still happened, but they stayed in the bar where they could be supervised by the employees. For example, his crew was on the left side of the second floor while the crew from Grenoria was on the right side of the third floor. That arrangement eliminated the chances for the two groups to interact. It was smart, and Mel had to applaud the staff for thinking of it in the first place.

Imogene was in room 22. Mel knocked on the wooden door. "I'm not coming down, so stop trying! I'm sick!" she called from inside.

Imogene…. You are a horrible liar. Mel winced. "It's Mel. Please let me in, we need to talk," he told her.

There was the sound of movement from the other

side of the door, and then slowly the door opened. Imogene was a tall woman, with ocher brown skin and a tightly coiled afro. She was muscular from all of her time on the ship. Imogene didn't have bones, or organs for that matter. Patches of her skin were missing, and Mel could see right through to the bee hive that was the interior of her body. She was a hive. A living breathing bee hive to be specific.

"Mel! It's nice to see you. Come in quickly, though. We don't know who's watching," she smiled.

The room was nice, but to be honest the Mel's view of nice was warped. He had lived in literal caves during the war with Grenoria, and now anything with four walls seemed fancy to him. So actually, it was a pretty average inn. Just a plain wooden bed, a window, and a small wooden table with two chairs. Mel took a seat on one of the chairs, while Imogene sat on the bed.

"As glad as I am to see you, I have a feeling this isn't a social call," she stated.

Mel nodded. "I'm giving you a warning to be careful. Have you noticed anything weird here?"

"I have actually. I've been getting more stares here then normal. A lot more. It's like they've never even seen a hive."

"Has anyone approached you?" he inquired.

She waved him off. "A couple small children, but they were called back by their parents."

Mel sighed. "That's good. Very good, actually."

"I suppose you know what all of this is about?" she asked.

"I do," he confirmed. "It's not a pretty story, I'll warn you."

She frowned, and her bees all landed so the buzzing would stop and she could listen better. "I'd still like to know."

"The last king prior to this one had all of the hives in the kingdom assassinated," Mel told her.

She gasped. Her bees flew up and started to buzz around the room frantically. "Yeah, That's not pretty. But, well, I can't say I wasn't expecting it. What do you suppose I do?"

"I'm not sure, to be honest. Your being very careful already. Not going downstairs is smart, by the way."

She smiled. "Thank you. I got tired of the stares I was getting from staff. I think I'll go stay on the ship. It's probably safer than on land."

Mel agreed it was a good plan. "Also, if someone from Carnelian does try to attack you on a Cerulean ship, it will be taken as an attack against the kingdom. Still, I'd take at least one other person with you just to be safe."

"You think I should tell the crew?" Imogen questioned. She was hesitant, and Mel could understand why. This whole thing was a very delicate situation.

Mel nodded, and she sighed and threw her head back. "I trust them, and I would hope you trust them too. At the very least, tell one other person and stay with them on the ship. That way you have someone watching your back."

She raised an eyebrow. "Is that an order, your highness?"

"No!" Mel backtracked. "I won't force you to do

anything, I just thought it was a good idea to stay safe and—"

She laughed. "Calm down. I'm just teasing. I'll consider it, though."

Mel stood up and made his way to the door. "I should probably head back now. Imogene, be safe."

Imogene nodded. Her bees all buzzed around Mel's head one last time before flying through a hole where her eye should have been and back into their hive. "I'll be careful. Is there anything else I should know about?"

Mel hesitated. "Tell the rest of the crew," he eventually said, "that there's trouble brewing. Battles on the horizon. Stay alert. I don't want any of you to get caught in the crossfire."

Chapter 14

Cassius was pleasantly surprised with Princess Audra. He had come here to help Athos and the Shining Sea Pod serve their vengeance. He had honestly not wanted to go, but it was his duty to his country. The one saving grace was that Mel would be there. He always loved spending time with the other prince.

When he had first arrived, he thought Princess Audra was going to be one of those annoying and bratty princesses who bossed others around and only cared about herself. That was the case for most of the princesses who rarely ever left the castle. They didn't leave because they had everything they could want in the palace. Instead, he found someone who could become a great leader. She was calm, and though she seemed to be run by her heart, she used her head to get her there. She seemed quick to anger when something was wrong despite trying to hide it, and she could handle getting a little bloody. He could see this all because he himself was used to acting the same way. Covering his emotions with a cold facade.

Having emotions wasn't a bad thing for a ruler. Having strong emotions can lead you to be more focused on your goal if you think something is wrong. It's showing them that causes problems. People might see your weaknesses. Your attachments, your goals. People can use this against you. That wasn't something you could let happen if you run a whole country.

Mel wore his emotions on his sleeve, and that wasn't always a bad thing. His happy energy made most others happy too. He lit up the room. He could only hope people wouldn't use his openness against him. Mel would be crushed. Cassius had vowed he would never let that happen.

This had been a problem for the now-deceased Prince Ajax. He had carried his emotions and opinions with pride, and he had ended up dead because of it. Audra had known exactly how to play to his desires and he had fallen for it.

Cassius wouldn't let that happen to him, even if it was an old ally he was talking to. You never knew who would turn on you.

He pondered all that had happened since he had arrived on the island as he made his way to the hull of his ship. He walked into a small room under the deck and locked the door behind him. Inside the room, a large clear orb sat on a pedestal. A leather chair stood facing it. Cassius sank into the old chair, letting himself smile contently before putting the facade back up.

"Ruler Athos, I request to speak to you." he said out loud. He didn't flinch when the orb lit up a bright, almost blinding blue. He was used to the massive amount of light emitted by the ocean orbs.

Inside the orb, Ruler Athos's face appeared. Their regal silhouette replaced the blinding light. "Ah, young prince. What is it you require today?" they asked in their wise-sounding voice.

Cassius straightened up in his seat. "It is not actually I who require your assistance," he informed the siren.

Athos's eyes widened. "Then who?"

"I assume you remember the siren you told me about in our conversation two days ago?" When Athos nodded, Cassius continued. "Well, some very interesting developments have been made with them. Yesterday evening, they were captured by the knights of Carnelian."

Athos clenched their jaw. "Oh, gods. And he was so young, too. I assume he's dead then?"

"Actually, no." The ruler's eyes widened. "They've been captured, but for an unknown reason the king is keeping him alive."

"That would explain the storms. The waters are restless. We knew something was wrong."

"There is something else too. It has to do with the other reason the king is keeping Hali alive. As I told you a few days ago, Princess Audra is friends with him. Or most likely something more. He figured this out and is holding Hali's safety over her head," Cassius explained.

"That's... surprising. But good for those young ones. Not so good now, I suppose." The ruler paused. "You said someone else needed my help. It's Princess Audra, correct?"

Cassius nodded. "Surprisingly, she had joined the

revolution against her own country. They have the plan to rescue Hali and seize the throne, but they need someone to take control of the wall."

Athos smiled warmly. "That won't be a problem, young prince. We were already planning an attack. How soon can the revolutionaries be ready?"

"The plan is to attack tomorrow. We can't waste any time," He informed them.

The siren ruler nodded. "Good. Tomorrow night, we attack."

Lila walked into the cold dungeon, pulling her shawl closer around her body as she carried a plate of bread and milk down to the siren's cell. There were only two guards posted near the door, which was strange. She soon realized why when she noticed two guards posted every ten steps leading down to the magic-resistant cells. That was going to be hard to get around. Any person trying to get up or down would have to fight their way through all ten guards.

She could understand why the guards were wearing their winter outfits despite it being the middle of summer. The stone wall kept the place freezing, even though the air outside was only slightly crisp. In the winter this place would be unbearable. Carnelian was known for being chilly all year round and absolutely freezing in the winter.

Finally, after what seemed like forever, she reached the bottom. There were no guards at the bottom, the last ones being at the base of the steps. The light only came from the small windows, so it was very dark.

Lila grabbed the torch from the bottom of the steps and started walking down the cold hallway. The place reeked of despair, the feeling of never having left even after the people who had been kept here had died. In the last cell, she heard a panicked intake of breath and someone scurrying. Lila held the torch up. Inside the cell, a disheveled-looking siren was curled into the far corner, shackled to the wall by a chain around each of her wrists. Her blonde hair fell in her face, not fully hiding her green eyes that seemed to glow with the light from the torch. Lila grew concerned when she noticed that her shirt was stained with purple blood.

"Hello. Warren is with us," Lila whispered.

Hali's eyes widened. "You're Lila?" Lila nodded. "Audra sent you. She told me." Lila didn't have time to question how Hali knew that, chalking it up to siren magic for now.

Quickly, Lila took the spare key she had been given and opened the door. The key wouldn't open the lock around her ankle, so she couldn't escape with it. Plus, she had to give it back to the man at the top of the stairs. Lila walked into the cell, kneeling down in front of the girl who had only slightly eased her way out of the corner. "Are you hurtin'?" she asked. Hali nodded. "Where?"

Hali gestured to her chest. "I was stabbed... I don't actually know how long ago. I closed it, but the wound reopened while I was running." She placed a hand to where Lila assumed the injury was. She flinched when she touched it. "I think it stopped bleeding but it still hurts. Also just a general ache everywhere."

Lila took out a roll of bandages and handed them to her. "I'm sorry, this is the best I could get. I'll have someone bring more when we get you out of here."

Hali nodded. "Thank you. You should probably go now." She smiled up at her.

Lila stood back up. "I'll be back soon," she told Hali and with that, she left.

Audra looked at her sword, inspecting her own reflection in the metal. It was late. She had been up polishing it for far too long. She sat on the floor of her room, the only light coming in was the moon, miraculously clear of clouds tonight, coming in through her open balcony door. Its reflection shone across the ocean, turning the tops of the dark waves crystal. If it wasn't for the moon, the ocean would simply disappear. A space of darkness, void of all light yet hiding wonderful treasures underneath.

She wondered where Hali stayed. If she could take a boat out and be right above his house. If maybe one day he could take her down there, and show her the world beneath. She wondered what it looked like. The water was so dark, was it just as dark under water? Or did darkness act as a cover for the light that shone from underneath?

She wanted to know. And she would need Hali to show her.

Audra looked at her own blue eyes in the reflection on her sword. They were more grey then blue, if she was being honest. They looked so sharp. They looked so tired. She didn't realize how tired she looked.

Tomorrow, the sword she held in her hand would be covered in the blood of the knights of her kingdom. People who had pledged their allegiance, their lives, to her. To her legacy.

She hated the legacy her family had created. One she never wanted to be a part of but had never been given a choice. A long time ago someone had decided to do something terribly evil, and it had snowballed into what it is now. Years later, she was still paying for their actions.

If she could, she would take the sword in her hand and empty her body of half of her blood. The half from her father's line was dirty and tainted. She would cleanse herself of everything evil that flowed through her. Her mother's blood could stay. That blood was pure, and kind, and everything the half she wanted gone was not.

But that wasn't something she could do. The evil and good in her blood had been mixed since the day she was born, and there was nothing she could do to separate it. Sometimes, you have to live with things that weigh on you, and this is what she would need to carry with her. It was her burden to carry.

Burdens are quite heavy, she knew that. And if she could carry it, she could swing it at a high speed and hit someone with it as well. It would make a good weapon, she just needed to figure out how to use it to its highest potential.

Her sword was sharp, and she knew how to use it well. The gods of love and war must have blessed her, to make her strong enough to fight for her dearest. They must be smiling down at her. Audra hoped they could taste the anger flowing through her veins. She hoped they could taste all the layers of rage she had been building up all of her life. Every little annoyance she could never act on added a new spice. She hoped it was the spiciest thing they had ever tasted. She hoped it tasted delicious.

Tomorrow, the sword she held in her hand would be covered in the blood of the knights of her kingdom. People who had pledged their allegiance, their lives, to her. She couldn't bring herself to care that she was turning on her own like this. There are more important things in this world than loyalty, and loyalty is something that is so easily thrown to the side. Audra felt no remorse now. Maybe she had, once, when the plan was first formed. But anything she may have felt had been burned by the fire running through her veins. Maybe that made her evil herself. Maybe it made her a monster. She couldn't bring herself to care.

Audra was a fire. A blaze that had finally been lit. Hali was water, cool, and soft in a way Audra could never be. For a fire to love water was a dangerous game. Water was so much stronger in the face of a flame. One wrong move and the water would put out the fire. Similarly, if the fire burned too bright the water would boil. That had been their fate, Audra and Hali. The two could never touch, for fear of hurting the other. But things had changed. Audra had heard stories of a lake lit aflame. Audra and Hali would become that lake, working together to burn brighter than anyone had ever seen.

Audra took one last look at the water and vowed that as soon as this was over Hali would be back there. Returned to where he belonged. Where he would survive. Then Audra wrapped up her sword and placed it on the table, ready for the fight tomorrow.

Athos stood in line with their troops. Their general stood next to them, her eyes shining with rage. "This is it," she said into the still water.

Athos was sure their own eyes would look just as angry if someone were to look at them. An injustice was done here, and when they had first arrived the ocean felt like it was crying. Now it was silent. Waiting in anticipation just as they were.

Around them, the other members of their army were just as angry as they were. And even more bloodthirsty. They didn't need to worry, there would be plenty of food for everyone tonight. Athos could feel the souls of the guards, up on their high towers. They had no idea what was coming for them.

"Everyone!" they called, amplified by magic so the line of warriors surrounding the island could hear them. "It's time."

A cheer rang out. A battle cry, from those who hadn't made it in time to help. But they were here now. Oh, they were here now. And the king would regret ever trying to keep them out.

Athos looked up. The sunset's warm colors cut through the deep darkness of the ocean. The water around them churned with the power of thousands of sirens ready to fight. Against the forming magic, the small beams of sunset began to look like a raging fire.

It seemed very, very fitting.

Athos reached into their very soul and called fourth their power. It was an angry beast, one that squirmed and screamed to be let go. It wanted to destroy, and rip, and scream. It wanted to tear down any evil it saw. Usually, Atho kept it on a tight leash. It did not control them. But not today. Today, they let it go.

It flowed into to water, joining with the magic of the rest. With a final cry, they pushed off from the sea floor. Rising from the depths. Scary, like the monsters the humans thought they were.

CHAPTER 15

No one ever said waiting was the easy part. The plans were set, preparations were made, and now there was nothing left to do but wait. People in the revolution always thought they were waiting for a chance to strike. They weren't waiting. They were preparing. Gathering materials, recruiting manpower, and working out every possible kink in every plan and backup plan so that nothing could go wrong. They had been planning and preparing right up until the last minute. And now, waiting was the only thing Lila could do. Standing in the secret passageways that surrounded the throne room with twenty other people, all of them waiting for the signal that would put years of planning to the final test.

There were so many things she wanted to say. In stories, this was the part where some heroic speech was to be made. But there was no time. Too much planning. And by now, when everything was finally silent, she couldn't make a sound because they had to hear the signal.

They were packed in like sardines in the dimly lit corridor. The air felt like lightning, electric and tense. No one dared shift, too worried that their metal armour would make noise.

Lila had never worn armor before. She had helped Audra put hers on many times, but she had never worn it herself. She could see why Audra liked it so much. Even as she stood so close to the danger she felt safe. Secure.

In the throne room, the conversation had finally begun. With bated breath, she listened to Lady Willow, Lord Balloren, and Lord Andre started a conversation with the king. It was muffled, but she could make out most things. It didn't matter what they were saying though. It was just idle chatter to lure the king into thinking this was just a routine check-in with nobles. There was a specific phrase the revolutionaries were listening for that would tell them when to attack.

In tense silence, they listened, until finally. "There it is! Go go go!" Sir Warner cried, and a battle cry rose from the masses as they pushed open the hatches and barreled out into the throne room. Despite herself, Lila joined the call and ran out the door with her sword held high.

The throne room was brightly lit, with high stone ceilings and the traditional red banners of Carnelian. Two gilded thrones sat on a dais in front of high arched windows, overlooking the water. In the distance, Lila could see the beginnings of the siren army's attack on the wall. There were only two thrones, one for the princess and one for the king himself. The queen's throne had been removed and put in storage shortly after her death.

And there was the king. Decked out in his ceremonial armor and standing in front of his throne. His cold expression was scary, but his glare was worse. He looked angry. Angrier than Lila had ever seen him. And that was a terrifying thing because the king was generally an angry person.

"So," he drawled. "You've betrayed me. How smart."

Lila gulped, and pushed her way to the front of the group, drawing her sword. "Your highness."

"Oh, it's you. My daughter's maid," he taunted.

Lila didn't take the bait. "We will give you one chance, hand over the crown peacefully, and there will be no violence. There doesn't have to be a fight."

The king hummed. "Really? And why should I?"

The first blow was struck then, not by a revolutionary but by one of the guards who had remained loyal. From there, the army that stood so still devolved into pure chaos. The guards who stayed loyal, few as they might be, did put up a good fight. Carnelian had always been known for the strength of their fighters. But against twenty people with the determination to get what they wanted, they stood little chance. Someone could be the strongest in the world but without something to fight for, they would always lose.

Meanwhile, the king took that opportunity to swing at Lila. She barely had time to block, and even then she could barely hold it up because his blows came down with such force. Lila knew how to fight. She knew the movements, the positions, and the craft of it all by heart. Lila was a good girl, but that didn't mean she wasn't a strong girl. Her papa was a dangerous man, known as the Scourge of the South. He had taught her how to fight before her mama had decided they needed a safer life and taken her about as far away from her papa (and his influence) as possible.

But knowing how to fight and being able to fight are two completely different things. And the king was able to fight.

Lila held her own for what felt like hours but couldn't have been more than five minutes. His swings were strong and he didn't even seem to be breaking a sweat. Meanwhile, Lila was sweating hard and out of breath. A good kick to the chest was what eventually took her down. She gasped soundlessly, the air thrown out of her lungs as she fell backward. But she didn't hit the floor. Instead, she felt something grab her wrist. Hard. Hard enough that she screamed as she felt something snap.

"*Stop!*" the king bellowed. He had Lila pulled close, still holding her by the wrist that had now been twisted behind her back. His sword was pressed dangerously close to her throat. Maybe it was because everyone was tired. Maybe it was because no one really wanted the fighting to happen in the first place. But for one reason or another, the fighting stopped.

Sir Warner took a step forward, gripping his sword at the ready. "*Stop!*" the king bellowed again. "One more step and I'll kill her."

Lila didn't want to die here. Not to him. But she didn't want them to back down either. Not when the goal they had been working towards for years was finally so close at hand.

"Why would that work?" someone questioned with false bravado.

"Yeah! Kill her, see what we care," another person said. Though the quiver in their voice made it obvious it was a bluff. The price of being nice. People weren't willing to lose her.

"You do care. Because you are those kinds of goody two-shoes who always believe they're doing the right thing. And letting someone die isn't the right thing. Face the facts. None of you have the guts to take the chance that I'm not bluffing," the king pointed out with venom in his voice. And everyone looked ashamed. Because it was a hundred percent true. Lila felt her hopes fall. They would listen to him so long as she was in his grasp.

"Why are you doing this!" someone cried.

The king stood stalk straight and growled, "Why? Why? You have the gall to ask me why? Oh, I'll tell you why. My family has worked too long to make this kingdom a utopia for man, one that you all were so selfishly reaping the rewards of. You never had to worry about monsters invading our land and living in our cities because my ancestors have worked so hard to clear them out!

"Now. Here is what is going to happen. You will all make way for me to walk out those doors. You will stay here and wait for the guards to arrest you all for treason," he demanded. There was an outcry of disapproval, but they were all quickly silenced by the tip of his sword digging deeper into Lila's throat.

Sir Warner growled. "Fine. But you leave Lila at the door, alive, and we will give you a bit of a head start."

The king nodded. "Alright." And then he took a step forward, and the sea of people parted for him. Lila looked down at her feet as she was dragged along with him. She didn't want to look into their eyes.

They stopped at the door, and as promised, he returned Lila to them. By throwing her harshly to the ground. "You should know," he told them. "That all of this was for you. Without me and my ancestors, this kingdom would be overrun with scum and vermin."

"The avians and the hives. You killed them. You and your ancestors." Lila stated, remembering a conversation with Cassius about the lack of other species in Carnelian.

The king sneered at her. "So what if we did? You all should be grateful. This kingdom used to be run through with *freaks*. The kings before me exterminated them, so this land would stay safe. But it wasn't enough. There was one species they were too afraid to touch. The sirens. And what did their cowardice get? A dead queen. And if it wasn't for me? A dead princess as well."

"That doesn't excuse the slaughter of innocents," Lila told him.

He opened the door and started to walk out. "They were not innocents. They were monsters."

"Even the children?"

"They'd grow into monsters."

Lila shook her head. "The only monster is you."

He laughed. "No. I'm a martyr. You'll see." And then he closed the door and left a group of rebels in stunned silence.

Audra smiled as she kicked down the door to the cell where Hali was being kept. It had only been a day since Hali had been imprisoned in the dungeons and she wanted her out. Now. Audra grinned as she kicked the first guard down the stairs. She was a bit surprised that there were more guards than Lila said there would be, but it didn't phase her. Hali was down that staircase. She needed to get down that staircase.

"You're excited," Mel commented as he blocked the guy he was fighting. And wasn't that strange? Mel is a fighter. She shouldn't have been surprised. Mel was the son of a revolutionary leader before becoming the prince. Of course, he could fight.

Audra smiled fondly. "Of course I'm excited! It's Hali," she said as if that explained everything. Mel just laughed and kept fighting.

Cassius rolled his eyes. "Can we please keep the small talk to a minimum? We are in the middle of a fight."

The other two chuckled. "Sorry, Cass!" they chorused.

Looking at their trio, Audra could see the difference in fighting styles they all had. Despite the fact that both Cassius and Audra had been formally trained, the difference was clear in how they executed the moves they were taught. Cassius's style was clear and methodical. All his moves are thought out and precise. His posture was strong, overpowering enemies with physical strength.

Audra's style was more fluid. Rarely, if ever, did she think out her moves. She did not plan what to do next. She tended to dodge and duck more than hit head-on, using the opponent's strength to her advantage.

Mel was a different thing entirely. It was clear just from watching him from her peripheral vision that he was not formally trained. His fighting style was more instinctual. The guards were completely unprepared for his unpredictable blows.

Between the three of them, they were taking good care of the enemies and making quick progress down the steps. Audra vaulted over another guard as she ran down the steps. She dodged anyone who swung at her, leaving them to be cleaned up by the others. She just wanted to get to Hali.

Eventually, she did, reaching the bottom step quickly. Cassius picked up behind her. She looked back. "Keep going! We'll get them finished up!" he yelled with a smile.

"Go talk to your girlfriend!" Mel yelled from somewhere up the stairs. She could hear Cassius let out an exasperated sigh from somewhere else.

Audra didn't need any more encouragement. She grabbed the torch off the wall and started running down the hall. The sounds of battle faded from her ears as she ran.

Eventually, she got to the last cell. She quickly opened the lock with the key Lila had snagged and went inside. Her heart broke a little at what she saw. Hali sat on the floor, curled in a ball in the corner. Her hair looked matted and her clothes were stained with her own blood. She was asleep and she was shivering.

Audra made quick work unlocking the shackles around Hali's wrists. She smiled softly before giving her shoulder a small shake. "Hali. Hali, I need you to wake up," she whispered softly.

Hali opened her eyes slightly. "Huh, Audra?" she asked, voice sounding tired and barely speaking above a whisper. Suddenly, her eyes shot open. "Audra!? Is that really you?"

Audra nodded and smiled. "Yeah, it's me." Hali shot forward, wrapping her in a hug. Audra could feel her body convulse from sobs, and heard the sound of her crying. She rubbed Hali's back while whispering sweet nothings into her ear, letting her cry.

After a few minutes, Hali finally stopped. She pulled back a little, looking at Audra's face. Sniffling, she said, "You must be a siren, 'cause I'm falling for your voice."

Audra chuckled at that. She stood up, scooping the siren up in her arms like a bride carried over the threshold. "Let's get out of here," she said.

Hali swung her arms around Audra's neck, making herself comfortable in the hold. "Yeah. That would be great. Not a pleasant experience. Here's hoping I never do that again."

"Audra! Hali!" Mel called as he ran into the cell.

Hali laughed wetly. "Hi, Mel!"

Mel smiled at her. "Hello, Hali. Are you alright?"

Hali shrugged. "Not great, honestly, but I'll be fine."

"Good." He turned to Audra. "We need to get going. Lila's upstairs and I think she's injured."

"Lila? She's the nice lady who brought me the bandages, right?" Hali asked.

Audra nodded. "Yes. She's a friend."

The group made their way up the stairs, carefully stepping over the bodies of the gaurds. Now that she was calmer, with Hali safe in her arms, she felt a little bad. They were just doing their job and ended up opposing her. Everyone thinks what they're doing is right and whoever's against them is wrong.

Hali watched them walk with wide eyes, making sure she could see their path. "So this is where I was. It doesn't mean much but it's nice to see more."

"What do you mean?" Cassius asked. He had joined them at the bottom of the stairs.

Hali shrugged. "I feel really lost on land. In the ocean, I can feel all the rocks and living things around me. It's almost impossible to get lost as long as you have a destination in mind. On land, it's completely different. It's like I'm floating on my own. I can't feel anything around me. It's weird and kinda disorienting."

Cassius nodded. "I've heard that before. Ruler Athos has described something similar."

Hali perked up at the name. "Ruler Athos? I've met them."

"So I've heard," Cassius told her, smiling the sharp smile that meant he knew more than he was letting on.

Hali scrunched her face up like she was thinking of something. "Oh! You're the ally they were talking about!"

"I am. Ruler Athos has been a dear friend of many years."

Hali nodded. "That's good."

They reached the top of the stairs, and sure enough, Lila was there. As Mel said, she was cradling her right arm gingerly. Sir Warner was also there. Not injured but very out of breath. "What happened to your group?"

Lila grimaced. "The king escaped. He looks old but it's a ruse, honey. He's still just as strong as he was years ago. It's honestly quite impressive."

Sir Warner grumbled. "The bastard—no offense, princess."

"None taken," Audra assured him.

"He's wicked fast. We could hardly keep up with him. And he fights dirty. Used Lila here as a hostage. That's why her arms were injured."

Mel pointed at Lila. "I knew it! You're injured. What's wrong?"

Lila shrugged. "It's fine, really dear, but I think my arms are either twisted or broken."

"That's not fine!" Mel chastised.

"It's not a high priority. I'll deal with it later, promise. We need to find the king."

Hali gestured for Audra to put her down. She did. Hali turned to Lila. "Where was he last seen?"

She pointed in the direction of the beach. "He took a boat out. I recon he's going to the main tower."

Hali nodded, face deadly serious. "Thank you." She immediately started running to the beach, tripping over her own feet and falling over as she tried to do so. She let out a loud curse as she fell.

Audra walked over, helping her up. "What do you think you're doing?"

"I can get there quicker in the water than anyone in a boat can. I'm going after him." Audra started to protest but was interrupted. "And before you tell me not to, I'll be fine.

I'm stronger in the water. I can take him."

Audra looked down and grimaced. "Fine," she gritted out. "But I'm following you. And I'm helping you to the water." She scooped up Hali again and started running to the shore. As they got closer, Hali could feel the ocean calling to her. It felt different, now. Stronger. Hali didn't know why. Maybe it was just that she had been away for so long.

"I'm good here," Hali announced. Audra nodded and set her down. Hali ran to the water, wading up to her knees before shifting into her tail and falling forward into the water. She had been right. Something was different about the water. She couldn't put her finger on what though. It felt just as welcoming as before. The dark water felt like being wrapped in a warm blanket.

"Hali!" Audra yelled. Hali's head shot out of the water, looking at her in confusion. "Just... be careful."

Hali smiled. "I'll try."

Chapter 16

Hali breathed in the salt water of the ocean, feeling its cool embrace soothing her aches and giving her energy. She had been away from the ocean and unable to access her powers for so long, it felt like turning on a whole new sense. It felt amazing.

Hali stuck her head out of the water as she swam, looking at the wall. It was complete chaos. Massive sharks and octopi made of water crashed and beat at the stone, making it fall and crack and break. She could see many sirens swimming inside the water creatures, keeping them stable. The guards on the walls were fighting back and killing some of the sirens, but the water creatures kept coming.

Hali was in awe. Combat magic wasn't something the Evergreen Pod had been very strong at. Sure, people like Marni could get strong at it, but most relied on physical strength. The Shining Sea Pod, on the other hand, was fantastic at it. They specialized in it.

Hali dived back under, putting all of her energy into speed. Sirens are naturally very fast in the water. It was their natural habitat, after all. She pushed herself further. Even if the thought of sleep felt very tempting at the moment. Even if black spots edged around her vision. Even as she felt herself start to fall. She hadn't had much energy to begin with, and trying to go fast wasn't helping.

Her vision blurred, and despite her best attempts, she stopped moving. Her tail locked up and she sunk to the bottom. Her eyes closed as she slipped away.

"Wow, Guppy," a voice called from the darkness, pulling him up and out. "You sure are a heavy sleeper."

Hali opened his eyes slowly, letting the blurry shapes come into focus. He was in his bedroom laying in his bed. He sat up. His mind felt fuzzy like he was missing something important.

Marni was sitting at the end of his kelp bed, chuckling at his sleepy state. "Come on, sleepy head. Your mom's making breakfast."

Hali nodded, not trusting his voice. He felt like he was about to cry for a reason he couldn't remember. He sat up and tried to swim forward, but he felt shaky and nauseous.

Marni frowned. "Guppy? You feeling good?"

No, Hali thought. *Something's not right.* But he didn't say that. Marni was here. His mom was here. This was a normal day for him, so why did he feel so strange? "I'm fine," he said instead.

Marni raised their eyebrow. "You definitely don't look fine, what are you? Sick or something?" they admonished him while helping him up. Hali froze. Marni's hands were cold, not warm like they usually were.

Marni helped Hali swim downstairs. The house was warm, with lanterns glowing a bright blue light on the green rock walls. The floor was covered in soft moss that felt nice as his tail dragged across. There was a sound coming from the kitchen, the familiar sound of his mother's humming brought a smile to his face.

They turned the corner, and Hali almost cried at the sight of his mother. She was a large woman with short blonde hair and the same blue-green scales Hali had. People always said he looked like his mother, and they were right.

"Amonnie? Miss? I think Hali's sick," Marni explained, setting Hali gently on one of the chairs around the table. Hali sunk into the seat. He shivered. *Why was it so cold?*

His mother stopped humming. She set down the fish she was boiling and walked around the counter. "Hali? Baby, can you tell me what's wrong?"

"It's cold," he mumbled. "And I'm dizzy."

Marni perked up. "That was not a lot of words. What was that? Three per sentence? Amonnie, something definitely is wrong! He's not talking our ears off!" they teased, though it did nothing to hide the worry on their face.

Hali's mom frowned. "Let's get some food in you, alright? If you're not feeling better afterward, Marni will take you to the doctor. Alright?"

Hali could barely even make himself nod. Marni got up and came back with a blanket, draping it around him. It didn't help much though. He was still cold and sad. Really really sad. He could hear Marni and his mother talking, but to be honest, he couldn't understand what they were saying. Their voices were mixing with booming sounds and splashes and screams that whispered in his ear. Like they were coming from somewhere far away. If his mother and Marni heard the mysterious sounds, they didn't show it.

At some point, his mother put a dish of food in front of him. He didn't really notice it at first. It didn't smell like anything, which was strange because siren food smelled incredibly strong. But this dish didn't. Hali couldn't even tell what it looked like. It was weird like it couldn't decide what it was either.

Suddenly, he was more aware than he had been since he woke up. And he really didn't like what he noticed. Marni couldn't decide what they were wearing. Every time Hali looked at them they were wearing a different outfit. His mother seemed to be having the same problem. Her shawl and hairstyle flickered in and out.

Something was wrong. Something was very very wrong. Hali stood up, ignoring Marni's protests. "Hali? Where are you going?" his mother asked. Hali met her eyes and gasped. They were lifeless. Completely blank.

"Out-t..." Hali stuttered. His mother wasn't alive... How could he be so stupid? His mother was dead. But, how did she die? He couldn't remember. "I'm sorry," he told her sincerely, before swimming out of the house as fast as he could.

Marni called after him, but he paid them no mind. His head was swimming and he was so tired. Almost on autopilot, he swam to Marni's cave, not really knowing why but feeling his magic call him there.

Except, when he finally reached his destination he knew why. He didn't even need to look at the rest of the room to understand. Marni was dead. The trident embedded in the floor proved that. And he remembered how. Him starving, Marni going up to get a soul, and Marni not making it. He remembered the killings.

"That took you quicker than I thought it would, kid," a voice called from behind him. Hali whirled around. "I never should have doubted you. You always manage to surprise me."

"Marni?" Hali whispered. "But, no. You're dead. Mom's dead. Everyone is dead."

Marni chuckled, pushing some of their bright red hair out of their face. "We are."

"This isn't real," he mumbled. And like a magic spell, the illusion shattered. The cave faded away until it was just Marni and Hali. His was clear, though not fully. It still felt like he was forgetting something.

Marni's appearance changed too. They were clear now. Like, made out of glass and light clear. The only thing that remained colored was their eyes. Yellow, cat-like irises surrounded by orange. "Sorry for the whole dreaming about your family thing. You're really tired. I'm here to help with that actually."

"*How can you be here!?*" Hali yelled. "You're dead! I watched you die!"

"I know, Guppy, and I am. I can only stay for a little bit," they explained. "I've got a gift for your quest if that makes you feel better."

"My quest?" Hali muttered. His eyes widened as the last of the fog cleared from his mind. "My quest! Audra! I have to—"

"Calm down!" Marni interrupted. "I said I had a gift. You won't be late. In fact, no time passed while you were dreaming."

"So that was a dream," he breathed.

"It was. I'm sorry it couldn't last longer, Guppy. You figured out it was a dream very quickly." They opened their arms, and Hali hugged them. They felt real. He held them so tight. He didn't want to let them go. He sobbed.

"Hey! Hey. It's alright. You've been so strong. Who would have thought, our little guppy befriending the princess? You were such a wimp, you know?"

Hali laughed hollowly. "I was. I still am."

"What do you mean?"

"I don't want to leave you."

Marni smiled sadly and pushed him back so they could look him in the eyes. "But you will. Hali, you have to."

"Why?!" he sobbed. "I have you here again! Why can't I stay with you?!"

"Because you have people to go back to, you dummy," Marni answered. "The princess, those princes, Ruler Athos, they're all waiting for you."

"You could come with me," Hali offered.

They shook their head. "You know I can't." Marni brushed a tear from his eye. "But, I can give you this." They placed their forehead to his, and Hali felt the most magic he'd ever felt in his life flow into him. It was staggering, like having the entire ocean run through him at once. "Hali, to you we give the power of the Evergreen Sea Pod. With all our love, we give you all the magic that was taken from us. Use it wisely."

The magic dimmed as it settled into him. He met Marni's eye and knew it was time. Marni was starting to fade. "I'll make you proud," he told them.

Marni laughed. "Guppy, you already have."

Chapter 17

Hali swam as fast as she could to the wall. She wiped the tears out of her eyes. *Now is not the time.* She told herself. Rapidly, she saw the wall coming closer to her. And as she got closer she finally saw the full extent of the chaos.

Bricks crashed into the water, chunks of walls falling into the sea. She dodged, barely missing a rock that crashed into the water. But even worse than the falling rocks were the bodies that came tumbling in. Both humans and sirens fell, all with many wounds. Looks of shock or anger plastered on their face from when they died. Hali flinched away, not wanting to look at them.

She swam closer to the main control tower, somehow being able to feel that the king was headed that way. She swam quickly. Her pace was only being slowed by the falling debris from the fight taking place on the other side of the bars. The fight was intense, that much she could tell.

She was almost at the tower when she realized she didn't know how she was getting inside. Without thinking, she launched herself out of the water with a huge blast. She crashed into the brick at the top of the wall. She looked down at where she had just been. *Well,* she thought. *I didn't know I could do that.*

The ground shook as one of the water sharks finally broke through the barrier. It crumbled, and Hali felt a huge smile break onto her face. The wall was finally gone. That smile was quickly wiped off her face when she noticed the piece of the wall she was standing on start to crumble. She booked it across the ground, feet slipping as the bricks crumbled into the sea beneath her. She fell, but not for long. A large wave swept her back onto the top.

She looked at the water. She could feel it moving and churning beneath her. The siren reached her arms up, commanding the water to come to her. She only expected a small ball to answer. That was all she had managed before. But, to her surprise, a sphere of churning water that was almost the size of a house rose up to her. Her eyes widened. She looked at her hands in wonder, not even noticing that the water she had summoned stayed floating even when she broke concentration. *This is the power Marni was talking about,* Hali realized as she thought back to what they had told her.

She turned towards the door to the tower's top room and then looked back down at the waves. "I need something. I can't fight barehanded," she said, Not really knowing what to do, she plunged her hand into the water. It molded, shaping itself into a weapon before solidifying. In her hands, she held the most beautiful trident she had ever seen. The weapon was a coral green color and stretched to be about as tall as her. Its points looked sharp and the handle was well-polished. A large clear orb was stuck to the end. Other than that it was a relatively simple weapon, but after years of hearing Marni rant about weapons, she could see how well-made it was.

The ground shook again. Hali ran to the main watchtower, using a blast of water to burst the door off its hinges. The room was relatively large, made of bricks with windows on two sides and another door on the other. The only furniture was a large planning table and seven wooden chairs. There, in the center of the room, was the king. He didn't look at her. He leaning on the table, his face down in defeat. His fists were clenched in rage.

"Why must you make this so difficult?" he asked, still not facing her.

"This can all be over now," she told him. He didn't respond. "You've done enough harm already. It's not too late. You can stop this and go live out the rest of your life."

"This has been my life. All this work! All this time I have spent!" he yelled. "And now look at me. My people, misguided as they are, hate me." He raised his head to look out the window. "*Can't you see!?*" he screamed. "This was all for you! You ungrateful—" He cut himself off with a grunt.

Hali took a hesitant step forward. "Please just come with me. Peacefully. You're right, you've done enough fighting. Be done now. I don't want to have to hurt you."

This time, the king turned to face her. He looked at her curiously. Hali sucked in a breath at the hint of barely contained madness in his eyes. "Why? You give me a chance when I never gave you one. Would you really be so quick to forgive me?"

Hali shook her head. "I can't forgive you. I don't think I ever can. But I don't want to kill you. That would make me just as bad. I don't want your blood on my hands. So, please, just give up. Go back to shore and give Audra the crown. Please."

He laughed. A maniacal, evil laugh that made Hali's insides turn. "Give up? Give up!?" He kept laughing. Hali took a step back. "You have to understand. I only wanted to protect Audra. You pests took my wife from me. I refused to let you take my daughter as well. We'd been doing it for centuries, anyway. It was my turn to contribute to the final goal. wipe all impure things from this world. I'll make it beautiful and pure for Audra. You see, don't you? It's all for her. A pure and wonderful world, with no stains to tempt her," he explained, sneering at her when he called her a stain.

Hali sighed. "I do." She could understand wanting to make things better for Audra. She loved her as well, and Hali would kill for her. She already had. "I really do. But you've lost. It's over. What more is there to do?"

"Don't you see? I am so close. I've almost won," he explained.

"What? No. Your kingdom is against you, your wall is destroyed, your own daughter is against you. How could you possibly be winning?"

"The goal was to kill all of the sirens." He finally turned to face her fully. He reached to grab his sword. "You're the last one left." Hali's eyes widened. "To win," Hali got into her best fighting stance, "all I have to do is kill you!"

The king lunged. She couldn't beat this man. He was a

trained soldier, someone who had been fighting all his life. She, a siren who wasn't always used to being on land and never liked violence, didn't stand a chance.

She called up water into the room, bringing the water level up to her ankles. It twisted and churned around her feet. She jumped up, pulling the trident back to strike. The king raised his sword, and the two weapons clashed with a loud clanging sound. Hali used water to pull herself back. The king swung again, bringing his sword down with force. Hali blocked quickly and tumbled back. She swung her arm up and sent another blast of water to push him against the far wall right before he swung again

She stood up, noticing slightly how she was more steady on her legs than she ever had been. She got back in a fighting stance, seeing the king ready himself to run at her. "I'm giving you one last chance! Stop! Come back with me!"

He shook his head. "Never. I will never surrender. Not to a vermin like you," he said. His voice was full of cold, controlled anger and hate. Hali didn't like it. "If Audra hadn't met you, everything would have been fine, do you understand? She wouldn't be disobeying me like this. She would have married Ajax, with no complaints."

"Wow," Hali remarked, gripping her trident tighter. "Do you really think that?"

"Yes."

She laughed. "Then you don't know Audra at all."

Hali's eyes widened as he ran at her. She raised the trident above her head just in time to block another swing of the king's sword. It landed in between two prongs. To her surprise the king twisted his sword, ripping the trident out of her grasp. It clattered to the floor. The king was quick to kick it away. It didn't go far with the water on the floor, but Hali still couldn't reach it with the king in front of her.

The king lunged to stab her, and she propelled him to the other side of the room. She ran and grabbed the trident, holding it in front of her once again. The king lunged again, and she jumped up, landing on top of him, they both clattered to the ground. The king landed on his back, sword falling out of his hand. Hali pinned him to the ground, aiming the trident at his throat.

"Are you really going to kill me? Could you even bring yourself to do it?" he asked in a degrading tone. Hali finally took a moment to look at this man. He was old and tired. A crazed gleam shone in his eyes, but under all that cockyness and craziness was an ocean of sadness. The kind of sadness of someone who had lost everything. The light of his life was gone, and without his wife, he had gone mad with power. Wanting to clear the world of everything that could harm his daughter. Continuing a legacy of hurt and safety from bloodshed.

Hali wanted revenge. She wanted it so bad. This man had taken everything from her. Her best friend, her mother, her pod. All of them were gone just because this man wanted to prove he could. She wanted to kill him. She wanted him to feel all the pain she had felt. All the sadness, loneliness, all the hate.

And yet, this was still Audra's father. Despite all this man had done, he was still Audra's family. Even if the two didn't have a good relationship or any relationship, Hali knew it would still hurt. He was her last living family member. And Hali didn't want Audra to have to feel the pain of losing someone, even if Audra said she didn't care. Hali knew she would still care, even just a little.

But, this was something Hali knew she needed to do. "I'm sorry," she said quietly.

The king smiled. "Ha! You should be sorry. You ruined everything! Do you know how long that plan took to form?"

Hali smiled and shook her head. "Not to you." Then she plunged the middle prong of the trident straight through his throat.

CHAPTER 18

Audra nervously tapped her fingers on the railing of a small sailing ship she was on. Hali had taken off a while ago, and she was following in a boat with Cassius, Mel, Lila, and Sir Warner. Sir Warner and everyone else had tried to convince Lila to stay behind because she was injured, but she insisted she come along. Sir Warner looked pretty shaken up by whatever happened. She'd have to ask about it later.

From where she was, she could see the wall was destroyed. She had never personally seen siren armies fighting, but she had heard it was surprisingly beautiful. Seeing it now, she had to agree. Giant, life-like sea creatures crashed through what was supposedly an unbreakable wall. The creatures themselves were made out of the water but glowed in the dark night. Small dots could be made out inside them which Audra could only assume were the sirens controlling the creatures.

"It looks cool, doesn't it?" Mel said, a lot quieter than Audra had ever heard him talk. Audra nodded. Mel didn't say anything for a few minutes, watching the quickly disappearing wall. The water animals were really doing a number on the wall. There was barely any of it left. It had all been torn down, leaving the bars that had held it up poking out lightly. Some had already been knocked over. There were blotches where bits of the rock remained, but they were small and spread out. Miraculously, the main tower was still standing. Even from where she was, she could see something happening in the top story. It didn't do anything to ease her worries. Hali was definetally up there, Audra would be surprised if she was not.

Finally, Mel looked at her. He had noticed her still tapping finger. "You're nervous," he stated. Audra tensed, then nodded. Mel reached over and slung an arm around her shoulders, pulling her into an awkward side hug.

Audra smiled a bit before sighing. "You're right. Hali's been gone for a while. I'm worried about her. I... ugh! I just want her to be safe! I want to protect her! But I'm stuck here, on a boat, while she's off fighting my insane father." She dropped her head into her hands, sinking against the railing.

Mel rubbed a hand on her back. It was comforting, and he was surprisingly quite good at giving a back massage. "I can see how much you care about her. What you need to do is trust her. Trust that she's strong enough to protect herself."

Audra looked up at him. "You know, you're very wise."

Mel smiled and blushed in embarrassment. "Well, I don't know about that..." he said while rubbing the back of his head.

"No, you are. Don't sell yourself short," Audra said, straightening up. "Thank you for the advice," she said before turning to the other side of the ship. "Everyone listen up! I have a plan for when we arrive."

Lila and Sir Warner exchanged a look. "Before you say it, darlin', there's something you need to know," Lila started.

Sir Warner continued for her. "Your father admitted that it was his ancestors who killed the other magical beings. That's why there's none on the island."

Audra's breath hitched, and she could hear a gasp from Mel. Cassius sighed. "It's not like we didn't expect that."

Audra shrugged. "It's just worse to hear it confirmed." Mel nodded in agreement, and she continued. "It's not important now though. What is important, is figuring out what to do. The plan I have is rather simple. We don't know what's happening at the control tower, but once we get there we will head up the stairs until we find them. Then, if needed, we'll join the fight."

Sir Warner looked down at them from where he was manning the sails. "That's simple."

Audra turned her head up at him. "I don't have enough information to form anything more. The Shining Sea Pod took care of the wall so we don't need to do anything about that." She turned to face Cassius. "I would like to thank you for getting their help. Without them, we would have had to storm the wall ourselves, which wouldn't have been as successful as this."

Mel looked a bit confused. "I agree it needed to go down, but why was the wall so important? Couldn't you guys have waited to take it down until later?"

"Because of a stupid law, my father made, the wall cannot be taken down unless every noble in the kingdom unanimously agreed to take it down. Whatever is done isn't decided by the king or queen or ruler. And if the king or queen or ruler goes against the decision, they can be executed by the nobles and the council appoints a new ruler. So, if it wasn't taken down by an outside force I and anyone else involved could be killed," Audra answered.

Mel paled. "Oh."

Cassius faced Sir Warner. "How long will it take to get there?" he asked.

The general looked out at the water. "That I don't know. I lived in the mountains my entire life. I don't really know how to sail."

"That's okay!" Mel smiled. "I do know how long it will take." He looked at the wall, and Audra followed his gaze. She hadn't noticed how fast the wall was approaching. "Based on how fast we're going and how close the wall is, I'd say we have about five minutes."

Cassius nodded, and went back to watching the wall approach. Audra sighed and decided to do a last check of her armour while they waited. Everything was in the right place, just as it had been the last few times she had checked it. Lila wouldn't have let it not be. She was good like that.

Five minutes later, the group quickly piled off the ship. Audra wanted to charge straight up the staircase, but was stopped by a figure climbing out of the water. They were a siren, and one of power based on their intricate armor.

"Princess," the old siren said, bowing their head slightly. Audra did the same back. "It's a pleasure to finally meet you." They gave a familiar nod to Cassius and Mel. Then, they turned to Sir Warner and Lila. "I'm sorry I'm not aware of who you are, but we don't have time for introductions. My name is Ruler Athos."

Audra nodded in acknowledgement and turned to run up the stairs. No one said anything as they ran, but someone would occasionally fall behind to help Athos up the stairs. The stairs seemed like they went on forever. A neverending upwards climb. Logically, Audra knew that couldn't be true. It sure felt like it was, though. Every second they spent on the blasted stairwell was another second Hali could be injured or dying. Every second was another she wasn't there.

As they reached the top, She held out a hand to stop them from going any further. Audra had thought that there would be battle sounds, but there was nothing. "Is this the right door?" Lila asked.

"I'm sure it is. Weapons out. We don't know what we'll find," she answered. Everyone drew their swords and Ruler Athos held their trident higher.

Cautiously, Audra pushed open the door and was met with a sight she had expected but wasn't ready to see. All the furniture in the room was pushed to the sides. Hali stood in the center, breathing heavily and holding a trident. In front of her was the king's body, bleeding from a hole in his neck. The floor was covered in a mix of water and blood that seeped out as soon as the door was opened. Lila jumped up, but it didn't do much to save her from getting wet.

"Hali!" Audra yelled, electing to ignore the body on the floor until she could make sure Hali was okay. It wasn't that important, anyway. He would still be dead wether she looked at him now or later.

Hali turned at hearing her name. For someone who just killed another person, she didn't look too bad. Hali smiled when she saw her. "Are you an octopus? Because you octopi my thoughts," she said.

Audra breathed a sigh of relief and tackled the siren into a hug. "You're so stupid," she mumbled into her neck. Hali held her close, patting her back reassuringly. Audra looked up into Hali's eyes. She wanted to take in all of the details so she could remember them. She had never seen anything like them, and she thought they were beautiful. The whites of her eyes were instead an admiral blue that shone in the moonlight seeping through the windows. The irises were a brilliant emerald that looked almost like the actual gem. The colors faded together where they connected, making it look almost like a reflection on still water.

"Hey, are you alright?" Hali asked softly, brushing her palm on Audra's cheek.

"Why wouldn't I be alright?" Audra asked. "I should be asking you that question. You're the one who just fought somebody."

Hali giggled at that. A sound that made Audra's heart flutter. "Audra, I think you're forgetting that I'm a siren. I've killed people before. This isn't exactly something new. I will say that fighting is a lot more thrilling than I had imagined. I should do it more often."

"Oh," Audra said, feeling a bit dumb. She perked up. "If you need a sparring partner I'd be more than willing to spar with you."

Hali smiled. "I'll take you up on that later. But for now," her eyes darkened, "are you sure you're alright? I mean, your father just died."

Audra looked down at the body behind Hali. She wasn't affected by the blood. She had seen plenty of it in tournaments. But she still felt bad. She wouldn't call it grief. If she had to put a name to it she would call it guilt. She couldn't really grieve for her father. She hadn't been close enough to him to feel any real remorse, but she felt guilty. Guilty for what exactly, she didn't know. "I'll be fine. Eventually."

From behind them, Sir Warner cleared his throat. Both Audra and Hali whipped their heads around. Everyone else was awkwardly standing in the doorway. "How long have you guys been there?" Hali asked, chuckling at the awkwardness.

"The entire time," Cassius deadpanned. Hali laughed.

Ruler Athos knew they had made the right choice. They could see the love in the eyes of the young siren as she looked at the princess, and they thanked the gods for the warnings they gave that stopped them from taking the princess away from her. With the power they could feel lingering around Hali, they were doubly thankful. Sirens are vengeful creatures, and even if the Shining Sea Pod came with good intentions they knew she would not take Audra's death lightly. Ruler Athos didn't think their pod could defeat someone with that much power who was angry, even when they had little training.

None of the adults, them included, said anything when the four children left the room. They were children, even if they were royals and experienced fighters. Athos themselves nearly quadrupled them in age, so there was no question. They were babies, really. So young. Too young. The blond-haired human girl, whose name Athos didn't know stayed, despite looking only a little bit older than the children. Athos had heard the man call her general though, so they didn't say anything.

All three of them looked at the body on the floor. No one said anything for a moment and then the blond girl walked over and kicked it hard with her foot. "That's for breaking my arm," she mumbled.

"What should we do with it?" the man asked.

"Gods if I know. I'm just glad he's gone, is all. That's what's important here," she answered, with an accent Athos didn't recognize. *She must be from somewhere inland,* they thought.

"I'm sorry if this is an inopportune time," they started. "But may I ask your names?"

The man turned to them and gave a slight bow. Not a full bow, as that was reserved for the rulers of the kingdom they lived in, but it was enough to show they acknowledged him as a ruler. "My name is Warner. It's a pleasure to meet you."

"I'm Lila." The blond girl gave a slight curtsy. "I'm Princess Audra's maid."

"Don't sell yourself short, General," the man, Warner, told her. He turned back to Athos. "Lila here is the leader of our revolution."

Ah. That makes sense. "Well then," they told Lila, "a pleasure to meet you, General."

Lila blushed. "Not you too, now."

"There is still a body on the floor," Warner pointed out.

Lila's breath hitched. "Yes. I suppose there is."

"Will the people want to have a funeral for him?" Athos asked them both. They weren't a citizen of this kingdom, and they didn't know what would be best in this situation. In truth, they had yet to even step foot on Carnelians soil.

Lila and Warner looked at each other, having a silent conversation that they couldn't decipher. That was fine. Athos didn't need to know their decision process, they just needed an answer. "They'll want proof he's gone. Won't believe it until they see it with their own two eyes."

"And it'll calm down the nobles if we give him a proper burial. We don't need to fight them and their supporters as well," Warner added.

Athos sighed. They had wanted to let him rot in this horrible tower. To not even give him an ounce of glory even in death. He hadn't given the Evergreen Sea Pod any glory. No, he had let them rot in the water, leaving their limp bodies floating for their families to find. And then killing the families who came up to try and take the bodies to have a proper funeral. It was dispicable. A terrible insult to the dead. But, this wasn't their decision to make. It should have been young Hali's, but they were in no condition to decide on something so big as this. Besides, they shouldn't have to make a decision like that at all. So the decision fell to these two, and they had chosen. Athos didn't have to like it, they just had to accept it.

"I will have my people bring his body to shore, then," they told them. The other two nodded.

"So…" Warner started. "What now? We've won."

Lila smiled, and breathed a heavy sigh of relief. "We've won. They're all safe."

"All?" Athos asked.

"Audra and that Hali girl she loves. They're safe now, from him. He won't be bothering them again. They're free to love each other, truly free," she explained.

Athos had to agree. They were both safe now, even if it had never occurred to Athos that the princess could have been in danger as well. They should have realised as soon as people started telling them about how Princess Audra was good. But no. They had blinders on. To focused on protecting their own kind, and getting a siren child out from the giant cage they were stuck in. They supposed it had to have been hard for the princess, living with such an evil man. But that didn't matter now. They were both safe and free.

"We should get going," Warner said, interrupting the contemplative silence that had fallen over the group. "The kids are probably waiting for us on the boat. At least I hope they are. It's entirely possible they left without us."

Lila laughed. "The dears were so absorbed in each other. I doubt they even noticed we didn't come after them." She sobered up, and turned to Athos. "You will bring the body back, right?" she asked, though it sounded more like a threat.

Athos nodded. "I will. Run along now, both of you. I look forward to seeing you again."

"We'll meet again?" Lila asked.

"Yes. We will. The alliance between Carnelian and the Shinning Sea Pod will be prosperous."

Warner laughed. "I'm glad! I'm glad. Lila, let's go."

They both bowed again and turned away to leave. "Oh. And Lila?" Athos called.

Lila turned back around. "Hm?"

"Take care of that girl," they told her. "She will do great things."

Lila's face turned serious, and she nodded like she had been given the most important quest in the world. *To her,* Athos thought. *It probably is.*

"I will. Don't doubt it."

Hali sat on the beach, halfway in the water, and stared at the sunrise. It had been only a few hours since the castle was fully sieged and the king died, but he couldn't sleep. He hadn't wanted to wake anyone up so he came out here to think.

The water was calming, though it felt more charged than before. Ruler Athos had explained what they thought happened. His fallen pod had made a connection with him, something Hali had never heard of happening before. In doing this, it raised Hali's awareness of the ocean's presence. He now felt the ocean and knew what it wanted. Whatever had happened, Hali was now one of the most powerful sirens in the North Ocean. That was a strange thing to think about.

The sound of sloshing in the water caught his attention. He looked up, only to see Audra cautiously sit down in the water next to him. "Dear gods, that's cold! How on earth do you deal with this?" she asked, shivering a bit.

Hali smiled lightly and shrugged. "I guess I'm just used to it. I mean, I do live in water. This is about the warmest it gets. Here, let me try something," he said. He lifted his hand up, willing the water temperature around them to rise.

"That feels so much better. Thank you," Audra said with a smile.

"Couldn't sleep?" Hali asked.

Audra shook her head. "No."

"Want to talk about it?" he asked.

Audra smirked at him. "Only if you tell me what's on your mind."

The siren rolled his eyes. "Fine. You first."

Audra leaned back and looked up. "I'm queen now. That's... big. And, if I'm being honest, daunting. It's a lot of responsibility. It's something I've wanted since I was little. What if I let the people down? What if they don't like me?"

Hali leaned onto her, resting his head on her shoulder. "Audra, you're wonderful. You're a wonderful person and I don't think you will let the people down. There will be those who don't like you. There always will be. But you don't need to listen to them. Do what you think is right, and the people will follow you."

Audra smiled at him. "Thanks. I really needed to

hear that."

"Anytime," Hali replied.

"Now it's your turn. What's on your mind?" Audra asked.

Hali stopped leaning on the new queen, choosing to look at the sunrise again. "I don't know where to go," Hali admitted. "I don't really know what to do. I guess I never thought that far ahead. And now that I have this power, I feel like I should do something with it. But I don't know."

"Do you have any ideas?" Audra asked, her voice soft and soothing.

Hali nodded. "Back before…" He waved one of his hands around, gesturing to pretty much everything, "*this*, Ruler Athos had said I could come live with their pod. I might still take them up on that. I miss being a part of a pod. But I also want to travel. See what's out there. Find other pods and try to help them if they need it. But I also want to stay here with you. It's all just so confusing."

Audra draped one of her arms around Hali and rubbed comforting circles into his back. "We talked about this earlier. As long as you're happy, I'll be happy. We've got the necklaces so we could stay connected. Whatever you decide to do, I'll support you." She looked away, a bit embarrassed. "I don't want you to leave. Not yet, at least. I don't really understand why, but I just feel so open around you. I feel like I can be completely honest with you. It's nice. Right now, I really need someone I can trust. The next few months are going to be hectic. Planning the coronation, reforming the council, settling alliances, and adjusting and getting rid of my father's old laws. I need someone to help me through all this. I need you. I've got Lila, I trust her, but it's not the same. I want you to be there."

Hali hummed in understanding, snuggling closer to the brown-haired girl. "I'm going to stay." Audra was surprised at that. "Maybe not forever, but at least until things settle down. I'll be able to find the Shining Sea Pod if I need to. And it gives me more time to decide. Maybe later I'll travel. Maybe I'll find other sirens to come back here and restart the Evergreen Pod. But we'll figure it out later. I've got you right now, and I'm not leaving anytime soon."

Audra smiled at that. She decided to change the topic a bit. "Mel and Cassius will have to leave soon, but they both said they'll stay in contact. The alliances with Cerulean and Aureolin are stronger than ever, and I think I could call them friends now. Ruler Athos will probably go home with the rest of the Shining Sea Pod soon. Most likely whenever Cassius leaves. I want to make good on a promise I made to my knights and start trying to regain peace in the mountains. I'll put the four of them in charge of that. I'll also need to redo the council. Lila's going on it, that's for sure. I might even make her a leader of the army. I'll need to decide on others though. I'd like to have you on the council, if you wanted to."

Hali nodded. "I would love to be on the council. I give great advice," he boasted. Audra laughed at that. "Hey, Audra?" he asked, getting a hum in response. "Can I kiss you?"

Audra smiled. "I was hoping you'd ask."

Hali kissed her gently, and at that moment they both

knew it would all be alright. They had had problems from the start. Big ones. And they'd solved them. That didn't mean they didn't have problems now. It just meant that the problems weren't life-threatening anymore. They still had things they needed to tackle, and that's alright. They would solve them. Together. It would be hard, but they didn't need to fix things on their own anymore. They didn't need to be alone anymore. And as long as they had each other, everything would be alright.

T.G. SPARKS *(He/Him)* is a trans author who enjoys writing fantasy and science fiction. His work has been featured in *Misty Mint magazine Vol. 1*. In his free time he enjoys gaming, streaming, going on walks, and taking care of his Axolotl Levi.

www.ingramcontent.com/pod-product-compliance
Lightning Source LLC
Chambersburg PA
CBHW071527120726
47907CB00013B/1102